ACROSS THE DARK HORIZON

Praise for the works of Tagan Shepard

Visiting Hours

Professor Alison Reynolds is an academic with a teaching career at Virginia Commonwealth University (VCU) in Richmond. Her best friend, Beth, is in the university hospital due to complications with her second pregnancy, bringing Alison for a visit, and giving the story its title, *Visiting Hours*. The visits will start an unexpected stream of life-changing events for Alison. Dr. Jess Baker is an up-and-coming doctor, new to VCU, who has recently been recruited from Portland, Oregon… the story about these female characters is solely about them and their feelings for one another—and the main characters' initial encounters are entertaining and heartwarming. Jess is charming with a bit of rogue-flare, yet she shows a sensitive, daunted side when interacting with Ali. For her part, Ali puts up a defensive front that's difficult for her to overcome, but when she does, dealing with her feelings makes for some well-written, emotional scenes. *Visiting Hours* is an emotional tale filled with denial, pain, struggle, commitment, and finally, more than one kind of deep, abiding love.

- Lambda Literary Review

The writing overall really was great, very impressive for a debut. This is not an insta-love story which I really like. Their relationship grows naturally. What was really impressive was the chemistry. It is absolutely there and in your face, and I love that. This is an easy book to recommend for pure romance fans. I'm always happy to find good new authors.

- Lex Kent, *goodreads*

I liked to read a romance with a character who identifies as bisexual and who isn't portrayed with stereotypes. I liked the tension around Ali's reticence to enter into a relationship with a lesbian. The climax is painful and crushing for the characters.

I think I held my breath for several paragraphs. This is a good read by an author who has done her technical research (I believe she works in a hospital) which adds depth to the story. Jess and Ali's first encounter is one of the best first encounter scenes in a romance novel I've read in a long time. ... is Tagan Shepard's first novel I believe and I'm going to keep my eye out for her next one.

- The Lesbian Review

Bird on a Wire

This is the second novel by Tagan Shepard. I said for her successful debut that it is a sign that many more fine books are yet to come. I am glad that I was right. *Bird on a Wire* is even better than *Visiting Hours*. The whole plot happens in just a few days but with a lot of flashbacks. I am not a fan of flashbacks, but I have nothing against them if they are reasonable and well-executed, as here. Robin is a good person, but her behavior can sometimes be quite frustrating and contradictory, and the author uses that very successfully to create some fine-tuned drama and tension all the way to the end. With all main elements done well, this makes for another very good book by this author. Keep them coming!

- Pin, goodreads

This is a book I had no idea how it would end. It looked like one way, then another. Shepard kept me turning the pages since I had no idea. I will say I was very happy with the ending. It was what I was hoping for. This is Shepard's second book and both have been good. She has become an author that I will automatically read now. If you are looking for a good drama book with a little romance, give this a read.

- Lex Kent, goodreads

Other Bella Books by Tagan Shepard

Visiting Hours
Bird on a Wire

About the Author

Tagan Shepard is a nerdy lesbian who lives in Virginia with her wife and two cats. She has dreamed of writing a sci-fi novel since she first laid eyes on Deanna Troi. This is her third novel with Bella Books.

ACROSS THE DARK HORIZON

TAGAN SHEPARD

BELLA
BOOKS
2019

Bella Books, Inc.
P.O. Box 10543
Tallahassee, FL 32302

Printed in the United States of America on acid-free paper.

First Bella Books Edition 2019

Editor: Cath Walker
Cover Designer: Sandy Knowles

ISBN: 978-1-64247-100-7

Author's Note

One of my principal characters, Gail Moore, is a member of the Lakota Sioux tribe. The manner in which American society and the Lakota themselves refer to members of this tribe is fluid, particularly as personal identity continues to evolve in this country. In the past, the Lakota people have been lumped together with the other Sioux nations and so some Lakota prefer not to use the term Sioux at all. More specifically, Gail's parents are members of the Oglála and Miniconjou Lakota Sioux. These tribes are also referred to as Ogallala or Oglála Lakȟóta Oyáte and Mnikȟówožu respectively. I have chosen to use "Lakota Sioux", "Oglala" and "Miniconjou," the anglicized terms rather than the Lakotan, a language I do not speak.

In my research I read several books by and about LGBTQ and Two Spirit Indigenous people. If you are interested in own voice stories, I would highly recommend *Love Beyond Body, Space & Time: An Indigenous LGBT Sci-Fi Anthology*, edited by Hope Nicholson.

Dedication

As always, to Cris.
To the moon and back.

CHAPTER ONE

The dull, rhythmic pounding of Gail's feet thudding into rubberized metal filled the dark room. Her breath, labored and wet in the thin, dry air, echoed in her ears. Sweat trickled in a thin bead across her hairline, snaking behind her ear and down her long neck. The scent was sour and sharp. It smelled like fear. She ran harder.

The first blow hadn't even looked violent. More like a brotherly slap on the back. Still, her security guard crumpled in a heap. Gail picked up her pace in a calm, calculated escalation. The second attack, coming too quickly after the first for any possible defense, levelled the other guard, and there was no turning back.

Gail saw the reaction, though the whole scene played out in pristine silence. A half-dozen prisoners poured into the hall, mouths wide with mute shouts. With each footfall, the tablet playing the security footage wobbled on the display of her treadmill.

The real fight had started off-screen. Search as she might, Gail hadn't been able to find a surveillance camera that captured it. She had to settle for this limited view. While the attackers surged across the screen, disappearing through the opposite side of the frame, the prisoners that started the whole encounter picked up the weapons their guards had dropped. They checked ammunition calmly while the real action was happening elsewhere. Their smooth disinterest annoyed Gail. Her face pinched into a scowl.

Gail was running too fast now. The heart monitor strapped across her chest sent a warning to the treadmill and an alert flashed on its display, telling her to slow her pace. She ignored both the alarm and the scream of her lungs as she sucked at the insubstantial, recycled air. The time stamp at the bottom right corner of the video indicated that in exactly three seconds the next guard would enter the frame. She counted them down mentally, her lips tracing the numbers as sweat collected on her upper lip.

Her eyes flashed to the left of the screen, picking up the guard and tracking his movement. The black and white camera mounted ten feet above them recorded no sound when the butt of the prisoner's newly acquired rifle connected with the guard's jaw. Despite the silence Gail felt the crack of bone. She winced at the mist of blood, perfectly visible in her tablet's high-resolution display. For a moment she could even taste the metallic tang. The guard's eyes rolled back in his head as he disappeared from view.

Gail's legs burned past her point of endurance, and she slowed perceptively. The treadmill matched her pace and the alert finally stopped flashing as her heart rate dropped below the red line. On the screen in front of her, the action also tapered. Her guards had been woefully outnumbered and taken by surprise. The screen flashed from one camera angle to another with only a brief pause to show that those guards who weren't on the ground were retreating from their stations, the panic clear in their wide eyes.

The screen switched back to footage from the original camera as Gail slowed to a jog. This was the part she needed to focus on. The reason she kept watching the compiled footage over and over again. Anyone could tell that the man entering the frame was the catalyst for all this violence. He carried himself like a man without fear. A man with authority. A man with acolytes to do his bidding.

She'd spoken to him a week ago in an attempt to avoid the scene playing out in grainy footage on her tablet. After the first work detail failed to report for their shift he'd sent a letter to her office, detailing the prisoners' concerns. She went to negotiate and found him lounging on his bunk like a warlord, smug and sly. When she asked to speak to him, he'd shouted a barking, raspy laugh that spoke of years of hard living. What followed was less a conversation than a chance for him to stare at her breasts and lovingly detail his actions toward women like her that had landed him here. She could hear snickering from the rooms on either side of his as she left, knowing in her gut that this would end badly.

He walked into the frame slowly and stopped in the dead center of the room. Looking around with a complacent smile, his gaze fell on the guard with the broken jaw. Only the guard's legs were visible, but they twitched and dragged as he writhed in pain. The man smiled, then pulled back his stained boot and struck out. The guard's legs went still.

A prisoner hurried up to the man in charge and held a handgun out to him. The leader looked at it for a long time, tracing its curves and its sharp angles with an almost indecent serenity. He wrapped a large hand around the grip and lifted it from his subordinate's hands. The other man hurried off, leaving him alone with the gun, the legs of the wounded guard just visible.

Gail flinched in anticipation as the man's gaze went back to the guard. Every time she watched this moment, she expected him to level his weapon and squeeze the trigger. When he turned his eyes away, Gail again sighed in relief. The light moment was short-lived. The man turned his attention now to the camera. He stared into it, a smile forming on his lips and his thumb absentmindedly stroking the barrel of the gun.

Something in that smile made Gail's stomach twist with disgust. It was as though he was looking directly at her rather than an inert piece of electronic equipment. She did not want him to see her. She never wanted him to see her. When he leveled the barrel of his pistol at the camera, it was almost a relief. He held the gun there for what felt like a long time. She had time to look down the barrel. To imagine the bullet waiting at the end of it.

The shot came with a flash of light followed by blackness when the camera disintegrated. The video file ended and the replay controls popped up on the blank screen. Gail was a businesswoman, trained to look for the positives in any deal. The only positive she could take from this event was that only one shot was fired. Apart from one severely fractured jaw, the only permanent injuries were to the guards' pride. Even the guard with the broken jaw was safe, recovering in the facility's Clinic.

Gail slowed to a walk and activated the tablet's voice-to-text feature. She checked the glowing red digits of the clock above the water fountain. It was far too early to text, so instead she instructed the software to begin an email to her secretary.

"Please inform me as soon as the support team's plane is on approach."

Once the email had gone, she drained her water bottle. It was still very early. She guessed that she had two hours until her assistant would receive the message. The inbound team shouldn't be in range for some time after that. With a few quick swipes on the screen of her tablet, she cued up the video again.

Hitting play, she started to run.

CHAPTER TWO

Major Charlene Hawk had always enjoyed flying. She'd grown up on the lower end of middle class in the rural South, and her family never had the money for a vacation that included air travel. She hadn't even been on a plane until the Army sent her to the second half of her Basic Training at Fort Huachuca in Arizona. It had been that moment when she fell in love with the feeling. Not only the rush during takeoff, when the blast of speed forced her back into her seat, but also the sense of importance being on the flight in the first place.

She had been the only woman selected for intelligence training that year. The significance wasn't lost on her then and it wasn't lost on her now. Ever since that first adrenaline and pride-filled trip, flying had become full of expectation for her. She would board a plane heading to her next posting and know that she had another chance to prove her worth.

This particular flight was like no other she had ever taken, but the feeling of tearing through the skies was familiar enough to set her at ease. It didn't hurt that the seats on this plane were vastly more comfortable than those on commercial flights. The entirety of Charlie Company was on board, so there was no room in the coach section for her. In fact, more than half her Company was in makeshift seating in the cargo hold. She lounged in first class for the first time in her life and tried to feel guilty for loving the extravagance of it all. The biggest difference, however, was not luxury of the first-class cabin. It was the view through the porthole windows.

Rather than the cotton-ball fluff of cloud tops, she saw a vast blanket of inky blackness pinpricked with glittering stars. It was disorienting to see the empty void of space from her airplane window. Though, she supposed, she was technically in a space shuttle, not an airplane, no matter how much it resembled the latter. The engineers at Andrus Industries had inserted their new technology into the interior schematics they'd been using for years in commercial airliners.

Hawk had watched the endless news coverage of their breakthrough in space travel with the same detached interest as the rest of the world. She'd been occupied with fighting a war at the time, so she'd caught up on some of the finer points years after the initial breakthrough. She had marveled at the idea of drastically shortened space flights but was sure she would never have the opportunity to experience it firsthand. Yet here she was, reading through details of her team's mission while the Earth quickly shrank from view. She checked her watch. They'd boarded less than an hour ago and in just over two more hours they would be landing at the Andrus Industries' colony on the Moon.

"Pretty wild, huh boss?"

Captain Stephen Williams dropped heavily into the seat next to her and flashed a wide, toothy grin in her direction. Hawk smiled back despite herself. Williams had one of those contagious smiles with perfectly straight, gleaming white teeth. Matched with his square jaw, blue eyes and blond hair, he was the picture of the all-American soldier. Like Captain America in camouflage. He was exactly the sort of soldier Hawk usually detested because he was exactly the sort of soldier who could get away with anything, including the promotions she deserved, just because he looked the part. She couldn't hate Williams, though. He was a genuinely good guy and he had had her back too often for her to count.

"I'm not sure what you mean, Captain." She jerked a thumb toward the window of black space and stars. "Flying through space to retake a commercial colony on the Moon from a group of rioting prisoners. Just another day in this woman's Army."

The flight attendant appeared at Williams's elbow, all doe eyes and fluttering eyelashes. He took a bottle of water from her cart and turned away without a second look, missing her mildly disappointed expression as she moved on.

"Sure thing," he said, cracking the seal on his water and draining half the bottle. "It's more of an adventure than an assignment."

"I don't know about that. This could be a logistical nightmare."

When she tried to open her briefing folder, he slammed it shut again. "Oh no. You've been obsessing over this for the last twenty-four hours. Forget about the mission for two minutes and appreciate the fact that we are going to the Moon. The Moon!"

"If I forget about the mission for two minutes you and the rest of the squad will be dead this time tomorrow."

"We hamstrung the Taliban in Helmand Province singlehandedly. We got in and out of Fallujah without a single casualty. We took Pyongyang with barely a shot fired. I think we can handle a few chain gangers on a power trip. And when it's all over, I get to tell my kids I went to the Moon. Do you understand how cool that'll make me? Dad of the year, hands down."

Hawk set her jaw. She had worried about this sort of attitude but hadn't expected it from her second in command. This mission was just like any other, but the moment they start treating it like a movie starring Charlie Company, was the minute they were going to make a mistake. A mistake in Afghanistan was bad. A mistake on the Moon would mean all of them—including the two dozen civilians and fifty prisoners—would die in the vacuum of space with no chance of rescue.

"I need you focused on this mission, Williams."

He rolled his eyes and emptied his water bottle. "You're telling me that you aren't even a little bit excited to be going to the Moon?"

"I don't get excited about missions. I get prepared."

He laughed and slapped her on the shoulder hard but she didn't as much as flinch. "Relax a little would you? Just take a moment to take it all in."

He didn't give her a chance to respond before slipping back through the curtain to coach. He knew her well enough by now to know she wouldn't relax. Not until this was all over and they were on this same plane watching the stars streak behind them in the opposite direction. She'd been a soldier for a long time. She knew how to read a situation. She knew to trust her gut.

Her gut was telling her this wasn't going to be a mission like any other she'd been a part of. Not just because it was on the Moon. Something about it didn't feel right. It was like a rock in her boot, annoying her with every step and too far imbedded to be dislodged. Something must have been left out of her briefing. Something that would explain why this mission felt different from all the others. She flipped the folder open again, hoping to find what was making her so uneasy.

CHAPTER THREE

Gail Moore was the only person moving under the dome. Looking down over the open courtyard, the only stirring she saw was the gentle sway of leaves on the potted palms in the current of the air-conditioning. She checked her watch and saw that it was just time for her staff to be waking. If this were a normal day, the early risers would soon step out onto their balconies and look out over the last few hours of sunlight they'd have for a long time.

Today, however, was not a normal day. She doubted she'd see another soul until the soldiers arrived. No one felt safe right now, so Gail would no doubt be the only early riser. Not that she was, strictly speaking, an early riser. Closer to an insomniac. She hadn't had more than four hours of sleep a single night since she arrived on the Moon. On Earth she rarely managed more than six.

As her steps took her closer to the glass wall of the dome, Gail took a sharp turn down a short hall ending in a nondescript door. The ID badge hanging from her lanyard enabled access, as it did to every other door in the facility. It clicked shut behind her, blocking out the view of the wide, foreign sky. This was a maintenance corridor, complete with painfully bright fluorescent lights and dingy white walls. The floor tiles were stained and scuffed. She took stock of the disrepair as she walked at a clipped pace and made a mental note to inform Environmental Services. She didn't care that few people used this hall, every inch of her domain should be in order.

The chill that always accompanied that thought caught her unexpectedly, starting a shiver at the base of her skull and travelling the length of her straight back. Her domain. The people who lived and worked here were her people. Her responsibility. As always, the weight of that responsibility settled uncomfortably on her shoulders, like a too-heavy coat she longed to shed. This was what she had worked for her whole life, but it was still an awesome burden. She both loved and hated the power.

Her running shoes squeaked on the waxed tile. She turned another corner down a less well-lit corridor and tried to shake the doubt from her mind. Now more than any other time in her life, she needed to be confident in herself. In her place here. She was in charge of Moon Base, and if she didn't start acting like it, people would die. Her shoulders straightened as she forced herself back on track. Her thin T-shirt stuck to the drying sweat on her back. Her long legs, bare from the top of her ankle socks to the high hem of her running shorts began to feel the chill of the air again.

Gail had spent the last three hours in the gym downstairs. The gym lights were set to twilight dim until 0700, when most of the station would be awake and inclined to get in their medically required thirty minutes of daily cardio. That was about the time Gail finished her workout every day, today included. While the rest of the station slept, she ran. She preferred the low lighting and the solitude, but the exercise itself was as necessary as oxygen to her. The limits of Moon Base, its borders and glass walls, made her heels itch. If she didn't run she felt trapped. After her run each day, she'd walk the halls of the station, learning its design intricacies, checking its integrity, wandering her domain rather than settling immediately into her day. Today more than any other, with the shattering of her ordered world, she needed to monitor the station.

She emerged from the corridor into a very different hallway. This one was covered with deep royal-blue, plush carpeting that whispered underfoot. The walls were a rich vulcan gray dotted liberally with bright splashes of color in the form of bold, abstract art. The wood trim at floor and ceiling was solid cherry and gleamed in the sunken incandescent light. The executive wing of Moon Base was decadently generic enough to be in any corporate headquarters in New York. Only the view through the windows gave it away. Gail avoided that view as a matter of form.

Wandering the halls felt normal to her and looking out at the sprawling landscape should have as well. Gail had always loved to roam, had always loved wide open spaces. Her grandmother said it was in her blood. Gail's mother was Oglala Lakota Sioux, the youngest daughter of a proud chief. Her father was Miniconjou Lakota Sioux. It was from him that Gail had inherited the high, round cheeks that marked their people. Like him and her grandmother, Gail was the image of the great Miniconjou of the past. Lone Horn, Kicking Bear and especially their great chief, Touch the Clouds.

The irony was not lost on Gail. There were no clouds for her to touch here, she thought as she unlocked her office door. There wasn't even a sky. The wall behind her desk was one massive, unbroken window from floor to ceiling. This place was nothing like the place of her people. No clouds in a limitless blue sky. No sun on the Black Hills. No wind through the high plains. Nothing but chalky, dead mountains and empty, airless space. And so she avoided the view. When she was forced to look through the glass, she saw the broken-tooth skyline of Midtown Manhattan. She saw the emerald green, perfectly manicured lawns of Brown University. Hell, she even saw the barren wasteland and half-dried up lake of the Reservation. Anything but the dark, cold bones of this dead landscape. The lifeless rock of the Moon.

She shivered at the thought, crossing the room quickly to her private bathroom. There was a reason her desk faced away from the window. She did not like the thought of all that space. Beyond the boundaries of the dome there was nothing. No oxygen. No warmth. No life. On the other side of that glass was instant death. It wasn't something she cared to think about. She dropped her tablet on the desktop and hurried to the bathroom, eager to get the time-sucking necessity of hygiene out of the way so she could start her workday.

Her shower was quick and searingly hot. Steam filled the tiny room quickly but was sucked away through the vent just as quickly. The engineers here did not let a single drop of moisture go to waste. Each molecule had to be collected and recycled. There were thirsty creatures everywhere. Cows, pigs, poultry, people and plants. Nothing could be wasted with so many lives to support. An indicator light was built into every shower right at eye level. It flashed yellow when one's washing water ration was dwindling, then it flashed red as a final warning moments before shutting off. As Facility Administrator, she was allowed a marginally more generous water ration. Gail had never even seen the yellow light. She refused to take more than her fair share.

She dressed just as quickly as she showered, slipping into a suit with tight shoulders and a slim, pencil skirt. Her heels were high, but she was as comfortable in her four-inch spike heels as she was in running shoes. She was just sitting down at her desk when a soft tap on her door announced her secretary bearing a steaming mug of black coffee and a stack of folders under her arm.

"Good morning, Ms. Moore." She put the mug down in front of Gail, setting the folders neatly next to it. "Quarterly reports and the revised budget for your review, and I've asked flight control to notify us about the plane's arrival per your email."

"Thank you, Beatrice." Before her secretary could leave, she said, "Can you notify Cordell from Environmental Services that the west corridor on level seventeen needs attention."

Beatrice flipped open her tablet and began clicking the screen. "What's the concern?"

"The walls could do with repainting and the floors are scuffed." Beatrice's nearly imperceptible flinch made her continue, "It isn't high priority. He can take care of it after this mess is all over."

She should've known better than mentioning their trouble. Beatrice's body tensed from her high ponytail to the toes of her flats.

"You think it'll be over soon?"

"Of course. The soldiers will settle everything and we'll be back to normal in no time. You're perfectly safe, Beatrice."

She looked like she wanted to say more, but thought better of it and simply nodded before leaving. That would be the universal reaction, Gail knew. Everyone in her charge had volunteered for life on the Moon. Most of them had done it for the triple pay and radically increased benefits, but they'd volunteered nonetheless. They may be ill-prepared for an armed rebellion, but they were practical, firm people. They would be frightened, but they would trust her. They always did.

Gail worked her way through several reports, trying and mostly succeeding in convincing herself this was just a normal day. The prisoners would be subdued. That was the word the major had used in her introductory telephone conference yesterday. Despite the bad connection caused by yet another poorly timed solar flare, Major Hawk sounded like a woman who could handle their difficulties. She had a confidence Gail liked. When she informed Gail in a businesslike manner that she and her unit would be leaving Earth first thing in the morning, Gail found herself looking forward to her arrival.

Dropping her pen, Gail turned to her monitor. As always, her eyes slipped to the top right corner of the screen where a timer counted down, ticking away the time left until they crossed the dark horizon. When she first set the countdown display, she thought it would help her overcome her fear of the approaching darkness and solitude. It had only served to do the opposite. Now she agonized every day about the ever-present threat. When they slipped behind the Earth, blocking out the sun for two weeks at a time, they were vulnerable to so much. They had no contact with the rest of the world. No warmth and no light. They were alone. Cold stole over her now at the very thought and she forced her mind to something else. Anything else.

While they had the sun on their side, an array of satellites gave them a relatively reliable connection to the Internet on Earth. She would have live access for a while yet before the powerful servers in the basement downloaded the latest version of most websites for access when they were out of satellite contact. She took advantage of the access while it lasted.

A simple search brought her very little information on Major Charlene Hawk. Most of the articles were from a small paper, probably from her hometown, noting with pride a military honor she received in action several years ago during the North Korean Conflict. The accompanying image showed the woman she'd spoken to yesterday, but it must've been a few years old. One of those studio shots with a fake smile and a flag in the background. But there was fire there, enough to intrigue her. All she could determine was that Major Hawk had very little life outside of the military. She didn't even appear to have a Facebook page. Gail was very much interested in meeting her.

"Ms. Moore," Beatrice's tinny voice came through the intercom on Gail's desk. "The shuttle is thirty minutes out."

"Thank you, Beatrice."

Gail stood and adjusted her suit. She wished just now that it was a suit of armor. Despite her reassurances to Beatrice, she feared the soldiers would be with them for some time.

CHAPTER FOUR

Hawk had just refocused on the file folder open on her tray table when a hand appeared in front of her eyes.

"Major Charlie Hawk, right?"

She looked up into a narrow, friendly face. She studied the man as she shook his hand. He was tall, probably close to six and a half feet, but he couldn't have weighed two hundred pounds. He was bird-chested under a pastel-blue polo shirt and his long, knobbly legs were wrapped in crisply ironed khakis. The face was too thin, like a man who had just recovered from a serious illness. His cheeks were hollow and his eyes sunken, but there was a happy glint in the eyes and his mouth was wide and grinning. His hair was so blond it was almost white, and his eyebrows disappeared in the pinkish hue of his skin. His pathetically sparse mustache was similarly hidden by his complexion.

The rich, confident voice somehow did not seem to fit him. "Jacob Stone. *New York Times*. Mind if I sit down?"

He indicated the empty seat between Hawk and the aisle and was in it almost before she finished nodding. He leaned on the armrest, pressing himself into her space in that obnoxious way that reporters and used-car salesmen do to unsettle their prey.

She closed the folder and replied, "I wasn't aware that there were any civilians on this flight. Other than the crew, of course."

"Andrus Industries allowed a few reporters to come along and report on the uprising. They handpicked three of us. I'm sure they'll read every word we write and lean on our editors to show them in a good light, but it's something at least." He winked conspiratorially and set a couple of cans on her tray table next to the file. "Speaking of the flight attendants, I managed to sneak a few things off their carts. I was hoping for some booze, but they don't have any. So, I can only offer you a ginger ale in exchange for answering a few questions."

It wasn't a request. He spoke like it was a foregone conclusion that she would agree to an interview. She smiled at his impertinence and took a can, popping the tab. "That would be my fault. We're all on a mission here, Mr. Stone. I couldn't afford to let the men show up to an active rebellion intoxicated, so I ordered a dry flight."

His grin was more a leer than anything, and he only took a small sip before setting it down and turning back to her. "I must admit, when I found out Andrus was sending in an entire Special Forces platoon, I didn't expect to find a woman in charge. When I heard Major Charlie Hawk, I figured you'd be a guy."

"I get that a lot." He was trying to rattle her, but this wasn't anywhere near her first time through this dance. Her usual adversaries were far more formidable than this private-school weakling. She found that calm logic was the best response, but it wasn't easy for her to fake. "Andrus Industries did not send us, Mr. Stone. We are United States Army soldiers. We were sent by the Army and we report to the Army, not a CEO. Also, this isn't a platoon. A platoon is about fifteen soldiers. This is a company, which is comprised of six platoons and several supporting officers. Specifically, we're Third Special Forces Group Airborne, Company C and yes, despite my gender, I am the commanding officer."

At least he had the grace to blush at his ignorance. "Of course. My apologies. I should have known a major would be too important to command a platoon."

"Was there something I can do for you, Mr. Stone?" She patted the closed file. "I have a lot to review before we land."

"Yes, I'm sorry. I was wondering if you would give me your opinion on the situation up there."

"I haven't arrived yet, so I can't give you one. I will form an opinion once I assess the situation."

"That's not quite what I meant, Major. I meant…well, the whole colony in general. What are your thoughts on the…well, the ethics of the thing?"

"Again, I'm afraid I'll be disappointing you. Ethics aren't my area. I'm here because there are twenty-seven American citizens whose lives are in danger. I'm here to protect them."

"There are far more than twenty-seven American citizens up there, Major. There are twenty-seven civilians, sure, but there are another fifty Americans who are essentially slave labor. Don't you have an obligation to them?"

Hawk bought some time by swallowing a mouthful of ginger ale. "My obligation is to protect American citizens from both foreign and domestic threats. At the moment, those fifty men are a domestic threat. Beyond that, it's not my place to say."

"We all have a moral obligation to object if we see wrongdoing."

"Undoubtedly. However, you are asking me within the confines of my official capacity, which is a military liaison, not an ethicist."

Stone laughed, a deep rumble that was at odds with his physical appearance. "You're a hard woman to pin down, aren't you?"

"You have no idea."

He tapped a manicured fingernail against the plastic edge of the armrest. The noise was nearly swallowed by the hum of the engines. His voice was softer, less argumentative when he spoke again, "Isn't it all too convenient?"

"What do you mean?"

He waved his arm around at their surroundings. "This. All of this. The timing was almost ludicrously in favor of Andrus."

Hawk didn't respond. She knew enough human psychology to guess that he came to her to voice his own opinion rather than ask hers.

"Think about how many factors helped Andrus Industries become the richest corporation in the world." He ticked them off on his fingers as he spoke, his eyes flitting between his hands and the window. "They make this immense scientific breakthrough that speeds space travel from days to hours. But it was a mistake! They were trying to speed up their passenger jets to get an edge on Boeing and they just stumbled across interstellar space travel."

He shook his head and smoothed his patchy mustache. Hawk watched his zeal grow as the red crept up his neck.

"At nearly the same time it's announced that there is a global shortage of half a dozen raw materials. Gold, silver, platinum, nickel, even aluminum are just a handful of years away from complete depletion. So they sweet talk Congress and the White House into helping finance an asteroid mining colony on the Moon in return for free licensing of the new technology for government use. We're in yet another unnecessary war and we need the edge. So we ignore or bully our way out of treaties that say the Moon is the property of all mankind and within a handful of years Andrus Industries has a colony that is fast becoming self-sufficient."

Hawk finished her ginger ale and set the empty can back down rather more deliberately than she would normally have done.

"Only problem was lack of manpower. Not a lot of miners were willing to work in that environment, no matter how much they were paid. So they needed an alternate source of labor." He raised his arms to the sky in an exaggerated imitation of a minister. "Lo and behold the country finds itself with heavily overpopulated prisons and a shortage of lethal injection medications. Big Pharma doesn't want to sell to us because they don't want to be a part of government-mandated murder. They don't want public opinion to turn against them the same way it's turned against the states who still perform executions. Now we have all these prisoners that we can't house and can't release and can't kill. Andrus swoops right in and takes them off our hands. They sign a bullshit waiver, their families get a token check every month and within a decade the Moon goes from an abandoned, lifeless rock to a penal colony like Australia was. Now Andrus Industries makes more in annual profits than all the oil companies combined. And that's just the beginning…"

He finally seemed to have talked himself out. His cheeks puffed in and out alarmingly and his ears were red as stoplights. Hawk waited another beat before replying, "I would say the company wisely took advantage of market forces to leverage their product. It's not pretty, but it's business."

"Not pretty? Do you know how many prisoners died up there during construction?"

"I imagine a fair few. Like you said, though, they signed waivers and their families get an income. Better than rotting in an overcrowded prison for the rest of their lives for nothing."

He averted his eyes again, but the angry lines around his mouth were hard to hide. "How very pragmatic of you, Major Hawk."

"I don't have the luxury of being a crusader." His expression didn't flinch, and she sighed before continuing, "Look, I'd be lying if I said the whole thing sits right with me, but the bottom line is that this is a prison riot. These are violent men who were paying their debt to society and they turned on their guards and are now threatening the lives of not only their guards but also two dozen or so clock punchers just like you and me. They aren't the CEO who makes billions a year and set up the whole deal. They're regular people and they deserve to be protected. If there was a prison riot on Earth or a gang of murderers and rapists were threatening an office building, you wouldn't object to the police going in. This is just slightly more…exotic."

He opened his mouth to reply but was cut short. A flight attendant appeared behind him with that pleasant but emotionless smile peculiar to the profession and said to Hawk,

"I apologize for interrupting, ma'am. There is an urgent call for you from Earth. Would you come with me please?"

Stone snapped his mouth closed and stood, extending his hand to the Major.

"Thank you for your time. Perhaps we can speak again in the coming days?"

CHAPTER FIVE

Hawk returned to her seat a few minutes later and collapsed into it with a grateful sigh. The fingertips of her right hand pressed circles into her temples, fighting a losing battle with the headache starting to bloom. The mission had yet to begin and she was already tired. Tired to her bones with no particular reason.

She pulled at the lapel of her uniform, the bunching behind her neck smoothed out and some of the pressure released from her shoulders. She smoothed the front of her jacket and heard the crinkle of Velcro. Not for the first time, she regretted the Army switching from the old BDUs to these new Army Combat Uniforms with their pixelated camouflage and yards of Velcro. She'd spent almost half of her life in the Army, and she felt herself turning into one of the cranky old-timers who bemoaned the "good ole days." Not that they had been that good for her.

From the day she enlisted, she was forced to fight ten times harder for each promotion and for the modest respect she occasionally earned. When she did earn it, most people thought it was handed to her as a PR stunt or to fill a quota. One of the first women allowed into a combat role, she was decorated in two wars before becoming the first woman allowed into the Army Special Forces. Between the restrictions of combat roles and Don't Ask, Don't Tell, she had rarely felt like she could take a deep breath for most of her career. A man with her combat record and decorations would be a Colonel by now at the very least, but she had been passed over for promotion more times than she could count. She didn't feel the scars that had earned her two Purple Hearts in Afghanistan, but she felt the exhaustion of a career spent with her back against the wall.

Hawk closed her eyes and took a deep breath. She had a job to do and no time for regrets or complaints. She could wallow in her righteous indignation when she got back home. She opened her eyes and returned to the abandoned file. She flipped it open and the photograph that had grabbed her attention before drew her in again.

Abigail Moore's title was Facility Administrator, and the headshot looked like it had been taken for a corporate newsletter. It showed a woman who was striking, though not traditionally beautiful. Her skin was olive, her hair dark as the open space outside the window. She had high, rounded cheeks with hazel eyes that made Hawk wonder if she had Native American heritage. The line of her jaw was severe as was her straight, somewhat beaky nose. She was thin, almost painfully so, and the warmth of her wide smile did not reach her eyes.

Hawk was taken with those eyes. She wondered what the woman had been thinking when the shutter snapped. If she had any idea how haunting the image would be to anyone who bothered to really look at it. She pried her gaze away from the photograph with difficulty and prayed that she would be able master herself when she saw those eyes in person.

Because she would be the main contact at the colony, the first page of the file was a brief biographical sketch of Administrator Moore. The words were far less hypnotizing for Hawk. The ghost of her own career struggles lingered between the lines of text. Abigail Moore was a promising leader when she arrived at Andrus Industries from Brown University several years before the company's rise in fortune. She had worked hard at their corporate headquarters in New York City, and had moved through the company steadily. Her job title changed and her responsibilities grew, but Hawk had an experienced eye. All her moves leaned more sideways than vertical, and her titles revealed a reluctance to hand her any real power. She had joined upper management just months before the breakthrough was announced and was heavily, if peripherally, involved in the negotiations with Congressional contacts. She was perfectly placed and perfectly qualified for the promotion.

When construction on the Moon began in earnest, she accepted the position of Administrator. No doubt she thought it was a stepping stone to the CEO's office. Instead, she was still there three years later with only the usual annual bonuses to show for her success. Hawk had spent enough time being shuffled from dead-end posting to dead-end posting to see what had happened. She wondered if Administrator Moore saw what had happened. She looked back at those cold eyes and suspected that, if she hadn't known then, she certainly knew now.

Hawk flipped the page reluctantly. A summary of the current situation filled the next several pages. A photocopy showed the blurred image of the White House seal. What wasn't going to appear in this report but what Hawk had learned from a well-placed friend was the path this assignment had taken on its way to her lap. It had come to her superiors at The United States Special Operations Command, or USSOCOM, from the President's Chief of Staff. The Chief of Staff received the request for military intervention from the President himself, a golfing buddy of the Andrus CEO. The Chief of Staff instructed USSOCOM that the Commander in Chief felt the matter was "of the utmost urgency." If Hawk had any doubts about the reach of Andrus Industries, that alone proved the company's influence.

Her assignment to this mission probably had a lot to do with other, better-connected male officers running far away from what could easily become a political and media nightmare. But none of that was in the official report.

The report outlined a week's worth of rising tensions at the colony. The details were sparse. The memo was meant to raise more questions than it answered, necessitating immediate involvement just to assess the situation. Andrus knew how to manipulate with words. Even without details, she understood the volatility of the situation.

The prisoners seemed to have organized a work stoppage, and the laughably small security force had responded brutally. When a prisoner who refused to join a mining detail pushed a guard he was beaten into unconsciousness. Other prisoners rushed to his aide and shots were fired, though there were fortunately no other casualties. The prisoners were locked down without food or water for a day, which only fueled their anger. More shifts were missed, work ground to a halt.

Administrator Moore had reported in their telephone briefing how the previous day, the prisoners had overrun a security checkpoint, secured more than enough weaponry to constitute a threat and finally barricaded a key corridor, effectively closing off access to half the station. The civilians were starting to show wear and the security forces were gripping their weapons a little too tightly. No doubt the passing of ten hours had not improved matters. Hawk's CO, General Harris, had just phoned from USSOCOM to confirm it. He wanted an update even before she landed. Not a good sign.

Still, Administrator Moore's voice last night had been strong and sure. She stated the facts, frightening as they were, without the normal panicked civilian reaction. Before Hawk hung up she had known she had an ally in the woman with the cold, brown eyes.

CHAPTER SIX

Gail stood at the far end of the dock and watched the plane taxi to its docking bay. The room was a vast hangar with a wide, low airlock to one side. Once a plane landed, it would roll through a series of these airlocks which eventually ended in the hangar. Colonists called it "The Docks," and all resources and personnel leaving or arriving from the colony came through here. There were three docking bays, each with a raised platform to allow people to disembark while cargo could be loaded and unloaded on the main floor below. The plane powering down before her now was the only vehicle currently docked, and the echoing expanse felt all the larger for its emptiness.

The cabin door popped and hissed, disappearing as it swung into the craft. A flight attendant stepped out, followed by several individuals in military uniform. Whenever she saw soldiers Gail's tendency was to tense and stand straighter, fighting emotion inspired by the uniform. It was instinct with an origin she couldn't quite place. When she was a child, Gail's favorite uncle was one of so many tribe members who served in the military. He stood so tall, smiling down at her and patting her head. His boots always gleamed, repelling the desert sand that clung to everything else. No one wore a uniform like her uncle. He was the proudest man in a proud family.

Gail could recite her family tree back through Maggie Stands Looking, daughter of American Horse the Younger, who urged calm during the Ghost Dance Rebellion and was among those who favored assimilation. Her grandmother had reclaimed her Native American heritage in the turbulence of the 1960s, and she had passed that defiant spirit through to Gail's mother. The last time Gail spoke to her mother was over a crackling cell phone passed between the Water Protectors protesting at Standing Rock.

Gail guessed the imposing woman striding purposefully toward her must be Major Hawk. When they spoke last night she had found herself soothed by the timbre of the woman's voice. The sight of her had the same affect. She was tall, almost as tall as Gail, but broader across the shoulders and with a powerful build. The muscles of her arms strained at her uniform, as did her bulging calves over the high tops of her boots. Her gait was firm, the sand-colored boots clicking in a rhythmic beat.

Gail looked up into her face and saw an appealing determination. She had a wide jaw, but it as was as well-cut as a steel axe blade, with a firm chin and a thin, unsmiling mouth. Her hair was cut extremely short on the sides and appeared to be a golden blond, though most of it was hidden under a green beret. As she drew closer, Gail saw she had bright blue intelligent eyes that looked her over appraisingly in a moment before snapping back to meet her own.

Major Hawk came to an abrupt halt in front of her, the two men flanking her stopping a step behind. "Administrator Moore? Major Charlie Hawk."

She held out her hand and Gail shook it, feeling the hint of a calloused palm. She allowed herself a tight smile. "Pleasure to meet you, Major. Thank you for coming."

Hawk dropped her hand, squaring her shoulders and clasping her hands behind her back before responding, "The

United States Army is always willing to protect its citizens, no matter how far the journey."

The soldier on her left let out a little cough and Gail took it for the sign of dissatisfaction that it was meant to be. She looked to the soldiers marching out of the cabin door and lining themselves into neat rows.

"That's a very polite way of saying that my boss has friends in high places and forced you to come a long way to clean up his mess." She registered the amusement on the two men's faces before continuing, "In any event, my people and I are grateful you're here."

The Major ignored the quip and the thanks. She looked over her right shoulder. "Captain Stephen Williams, my XO." Then over her left. "Captain Jerry Forest, Logistics."

Gail nodded at both men in turn, and said, "I'm afraid I don't have anyone who can help you unload your gear. The dockworkers are prisoners and have not reported to work in several days. Their refusal to work was one of the first signs of trouble we had."

Forest smiled pleasantly at her. "Not to worry, ma'am. We can unload the bird ourselves. Mind if we take over your hangar here for our HQ?"

"Anything you need." She frowned at him but addressed her question to Hawk. "Are you sure you'll be comfortable here? I can't offer you all bedrooms, we don't have that many. Perhaps I can make arrangements for you to take over the conference rooms and offices. It may be tight, but it would be more comfortable than the hangar. It can get cold in here and the floor is just concrete."

"Not a problem, ma'am." Forest smiled a little wider, showing off a chipped tooth. "The Major here always takes us to the nicest places. We spent a month on a frozen mountain in Afghanistan with her and she got the medals…"

"Captain, please set up the Command Center before the rest of camp. I want a strategy briefing ASAP. That will be all." Hawk's voice was firm, but he winked as he saluted, nodding to Gail again as he moved off to the soldiers waiting beside the plane. She turned back and said, "If you wouldn't mind, Administrator Moore, could you show me the lay of the land and get me caught on up the current situation?"

"Yes, of course, right this way." She turned and gestured toward the exit, and Hawk fell into step behind her, Captain Williams at the rear.

She touched her ID badge to a scanner on the wall and the door unlocked with a loud click. She felt the heat of the soldier's body behind her and said, "Please, call me Gail."

She turned and saw that there was warmth in the blue eyes, despite the neutral expression. Hawk nodded and said in that low, rich voice, "Gail."

CHAPTER SEVEN

The trio stood at the railing of an observation deck hovering near the top of the glass bubble enclosing the colony. They had taken a winding route through nondescript corridors and then a seemingly endless elevator ride, but the trip had been worth it. From here they were able to see the entire complex, laid out before them as though they were eagles flying overhead. Hawk gripped the railing, scanning the view. Gail leaned against the same railing surprisingly close to her and described the scene.

"The colony is enclosed by a three-layered, reinforced dome." She gestured to the glass curving above them. "You'll notice the honeycomb design of the metal supports for added structural integrity. Each layer of the enclosure is self-contained and offset from the one above it, so if there is damage to one layer it shouldn't destroy the entire structure. All three layers are bulletproof and we are rated for a blast of up to five kilotons."

Hawk looked up at the glass just a couple of feet over her head. From here it looked almost close enough to touch. The panes were so thick that, at certain angles, they distorted the view outside. The layers of glass appeared opaque if she looked straight up, blocking out the stars in a blanket of dark. It was only at the oblique angle of their position that they could see through the far end of the dome, over a mile away at its base.

"We are currently standing above the civilian living quarters. What you see in front of us at ground level is the shared courtyard."

"Doesn't look like it's shared at all," Hawk said, squinting through the distance at the flat side of a honeycombed vertical wall that split the dome in half. Through the transparent barrier she saw a bleak housing block. "How blast resistant is that wall?"

"Comparable to the exterior though neither have been fully tested."

"I doubt we're interested in testing it," Williams said with a grin that Hawk didn't return.

"From here you can see the farming pod to your left." Gail pointed to a larger dome connected by a short tunnel to the main structure. "And then the livestock pod to the right." This dome was roughly the same size and shape as the farming dome. "We also have the mining pod and solar farm behind us, but you can't see them from here."

Williams scribbled notes on a pad he had pulled from a cargo pocket, and she paused to let him catch up. Surreptitiously, Hawk took the opportunity to inspect the administrator. Her suit was a subdued shade somewhere between light yellow and dusty orange that complimented her skin tone. Her hair was pulled back into a tight ponytail, exposing her long neck in a way Hawk tried very hard not to stare at. Instead she took note of the four-inch, peep-toe heels that were attractive but completely impractical for what was quickly descending into a war zone. She shook her head at the inefficient vanity of the choice.

"We produce most of our food here. Andrus sends regular shipments of items that are either impractical or impossible to produce onsite."

"Cheetos and ice cream?" Williams asked, scribbling fast.

"Essentially, yes. I insisted that we have some treats from home. You'd be surprised the morale boost from a few cans of soda."

Hawk asked, "Any of it get through to the prisoners?"

"Most of it," Gail responded coldly. "They do outnumber us significantly."

After checking that Williams was keeping up, she continued, "All food produced in the two agricultural wings is processed on site and then transferred to the two mess halls on the far left of the main dome. The work in the agricultural wings is all done by the prisoners, but we also have stores that can last for about three months."

Without looking up from his notes, Williams asked, "So there won't be an issue with short supplies?"

Gail stood straight and faced the two of them. "No, we don't anticipate that being an issue. We have water recyclers, so fresh water won't be a problem either. The environmental control is housed here in the main wing." She gestured over the railing. "It's to the right side of this dome, two floors underground, with no access from the prisoners' wing."

Hawk looked over the railing, her head spinning slightly with the dizzying height. The living quarters below her were curved, conforming to the shape of the dome in a step pattern climbing about three-quarters the height of the dome. Each staggered floor had an open walkway on its outer rim. Innumerable doors dotted the walls along the walkway. The design repeated ten times before ending at a wide open courtyard on the ground floor complete with potted plants and a tinkling fountain. A glass elevator ran along one edge of the walkway. It reminded Hawk of the only cruise she'd ever been on, with its glittering carpeted main deck and the endless hallway of cabins that branched off it.

The opposite side of the structure was vastly different. Rather than an open, carpeted walkway, there was a narrow passage wrapped in reinforced glass. It wasn't the pleasant honeycomb of the dome either. This tunnel was reinforced with steel bars so close together as to give the impression of a solid sheet of metal. There was no glass elevator, but a cold, steel box at the northern end. Some effort had been made to give the wing some visual appeal. The elevator shaft was punctuated at intervals with metallic sculptures in twisting, abstract shapes, but the ornamentation was for those outside the wing, not inside. It didn't take much imagination for Hawk to picture what the prisoners' rooms looked like. Undoubtedly they were very similar to their prison cells back on Earth.

She asked the question that had been troubling her since they boarded the space plane. "So, the environmental controls, is that what's providing gravity? How is there gravity here and on the plane for that matter?"

"I'll do my best to explain, but I'm not a scientist, so bear with me. The plane has gravity because of the speed at which it travels. That speed and the trajectory provides enough centrifugal force to keep you from floating around. The colony has gravity because of a mixture of increased pressure and electromagnetic fields created within the domes to supplement the Moon's minimal gravity. Either one alone would have to be too strong to be safe, so we use a combination of the two. There is gravity on the surface, but it is much less than on Earth. What we have inside here is actually only about three-quarters of Earth gravity, but it's close enough that most people don't notice."

Hawk bounced on the balls of her feet. It didn't feel different, but she had noticed that she wasn't feeling the nagging pain in her hip that was common after long flights. That old injury, from a training jump in airborne school that earned her a lot of teasing from her classmates and a click in her hip that she hid from everyone, was such an old friend that she barely noticed it anymore. If the lower gravity kept that ache at bay, she might end up liking this assignment after all.

"The oxygen is replenished with both chemical scrubbers and the plant life we cultivate. It was an expensive process creating the atmosphere and pumping in the oxygen when it was first started, but it's now relatively cheap to maintain with carbon dioxide conversion. There is no isolation of the atmosphere between the wings of the structure, so the prisoners would be killing themselves as well as us if they were to sabotage it. They do understand that."

"I see." The fluorescent light above Hawk hummed, and she asked, "What about power?"

Gail visibly tensed at the question. "That is our biggest weakness."

"Please explain."

"How familiar are the two of you with the orbital patterns of the Moon?"

Williams laughed lightly under his breath and shrugged at Hawk. "Wasn't covered in Basic Training for me. How about you, Major?"

She gave him a stern look and he returned to his notes. Gail continued, "Most people aren't aware that the side of the Moon we see on Earth is always the same side. This side, in fact. The opposite face of the surface is referred to as…"

"The dark side of the moon?"

Gail gave Williams a tight smile. "Pink Floyd fan?"

"Isn't everyone?"

She shrugged noncommittally and continued, "As the Earth orbits the Sun, the Moon orbits the Earth. But the rotation of the Moon is much slower than that of Earth. The upshot is that we experience fourteen straight days of Sun exposure before passing behind the Earth. Once we pass that point, the dark horizon, we have fourteen straight days of darkness. During those fourteen days of darkness, we function entirely on battery power that is generated by our solar farm during our Sun exposure. We have roughly two hundred acres of the most advanced solar panels known, and there is a bunker beneath the farm that holds the batteries. All of the domes are equipped with safe low-level UV lighting and multiple heating systems. Our power usage is immense during the dark time, and any failure of our batteries would be fatal. For that reason, there are multiple access points to the power station and multiple control rooms on the civilian side of the base."

"Making it more difficult to secure." Hawk nodded and continued, "We'll make that our priority. What happens if the power is cut?"

"Systems are prioritized in the event of power loss. We have limited on-site batteries that can keep us going for a while, but systems will start shutting down. Entertainment goes first, followed by administrative devices. Telecom with the exception of Earth communication consoles is next. Elevators and partial lighting. Heating systems go to reduced function. They can't shut off entirely or we would freeze to death within a few days. After that we go to emergency lighting only. Then living quarters are blacked out. Full heating, environmental and emergency communications and lighting are the last to go. Once the environmental controls go, a full population will have about four days' worth of breathable air. After that..."

"How long after a power loss before the batteries are depleted?"

"We've never had a power loss, so we can't be sure exactly. Theoretically they can last seventy-two hours."

Williams and Hawk shared a look. The time frame was ludicrously short. "Three days of battery power followed by four days of air. You're saying that Andrus only planned for a seven-day emergency despite the fact that you have fourteen days of dark?"

Gail began heading toward the elevators, the two soldiers following. "It's enough time for a rescue team to come from Earth if we can notify them before we cross the dark horizon. It was the best that could be provided for such a large project. Moreover, the limited time frame provides us with excellent motivation for careful maintenance." She paused at the elevator door, her back still to them. "I assure you, my people take the utmost care to ensure our safety. A rebellion, however, was not part of the planning process."

"Which also seems short-sighted, considering the population."

Gail turned very slowly, and when she looked at Hawk there was a fire in her eyes. "Andrus Industries sees this colony as an opportunity for our workers. An opportunity to reclaim their better selves. They are treated with the dignity deserved by all people despite their past mistakes. Treating them like an unexploded bomb would be counter to that purpose."

Hawk took a long step forward. "That sounds great on a press release, I'm sure, but the lives of you and your people are at risk because of poor planning. You can spin it for the media however you want when this is over. Right now we have to keep the prisoners as far away as possible from the power controls."

Gail's fists clenched at her sides. "They've occupied the prisoner mess hall and set up a base there. There is literally a mile of corridors between them and the nearest access point to the power controls."

Williams coughed behind them, breaking the tension and sliding the notebook back into his cargo pocket. "That sounds like good news to me."

The elevator arrived with a loud buzz. Hawk stepped past Gail and said, "That's the only good news."

CHAPTER EIGHT

At their request Gail escorted the two officers back to the hangar. They would need the next several hours to set up a base camp and coordinate responsibilities. The tension that had permeated the tour was difficult to ignore, and their goodbyes were brief.

Hawk watched Gail walk away with a firm stride and straight shoulders and decided that she had probably been unnecessarily harsh. In recent years, she had fallen into the habit of pushing her soldiers to test their limits. Ever since the worst of the combat in Afghanistan, she had wanted to know the exact breaking point of her people. It was a tried and true method in the Army, but perhaps not the best route to take with a civilian.

This particular civilian, however, seemed up to the challenge. She was calm and capable, and her defensiveness lacked the indignant pout one would expect from a woman in her privileged position. Hawk couldn't help but be impressed. It didn't hurt that she had also noticed the swing of the woman's hips and the slim curve of her neck. When Gail had reached to swipe her ID badge through the security lock, Hawk watched the ripple of lean muscle across her forearm. She mentally checked herself as the closing door separated her from the enticing view. The last thing she needed right now was a distraction.

She pulled off her beret and ran a hand through her hair. While it was short back and sides, it was longer on top and she wore it with a severe part on the left. There was something oddly comforting in running her fingers through the short hair at the base of her skull. She stared at the closed door and rubbed her neck, trying to bully her mind away from the pleasant direction it was heading.

The sound of boots on concrete below her brought her back into the present. She descended the stairs at a trot and made her way toward the Command Center Forest had set up in her absence. Her XO was already there, along with all the platoon leaders. She took her place at the far end of a broad table spread with floor plans and schematics. They were deep into establishing patrol schedules and engagement parameters before Hawk could truly say her mind was back on track. They hadn't yet met with the station's security personnel, but Hawk decided that it would be best to wait until after dinner to request an introduction. It would have to come from Administrator Moore. Hawk didn't miss the glint of amusement in Williams's eye when he implied that she would be best suited to sweet-talk the civilian. Before she could respond, one of the men came in to announce the Administrator.

Less than an hour later, Hawk found herself eating roasted duck and spaetzle from a bone china plate in the executive dining room with a woman in spike heels instead of a rehydrated MRE in the officers' mess tent with a handful of loudmouths. She would have felt more at home with the loudmouths. The meal so far had been silent and Gail had barely looked in her direction. Still, it wasn't half as bad as the ribbing she'd had to put up with from the men when she'd received the invitation. Forest had started it all with a joke about how it was the first time since he had met her that she was going on a date. By the time the rest of them got their digs in she had seriously started to regret her insistence on creating rapport with her subordinates. The thought of their jokes made her blush, and she decided it was time to start talking.

"You certainly know how to wine and dine your guests. Dinner is delicious. I appreciate you inviting me."

Gail finally looked at her with a brief smile that had Hawk staring at her plate again. "I thought you would need a good meal before I take you to meet Derek."

Hawk shuffled through her mental notes until she hit upon what she was looking for. "Derek Drumm, Head of Security."

Gail nodded and reached for the glass of wine she had poured herself even after the Major refused one. "Derek…" She swirled the wine and stared at it absently, as though the words she was looking for would be spelled out in the spinning liquid. "…remains unconvinced that our problem requires external assistance."

Hawk snorted into her water glass, earning a much more genuine smile from her dining companion. "Well put, Administrator Moore. They didn't teach me how to speak like that at West Virginia University. Tell me, is there a class on bullshit at Brown?"

"A whole semester of my MBA, actually. BS 101, How To Eat Shit and Like It, and BS 102 The Glass Ceiling: Getting Used To It." She took another, longer sip of wine and sat back a little deeper in her chair. "It is a women's college, after all, and they are realistic."

"I could have used that myself." The very corner of Hawk's mouth rose a trifle. "I've gotten used to being passed over for promotion, but it hasn't always been easy to accept."

"You can't have been passed over that often. You're young to be a major, aren't you?"

As close as she was to forty, it'd been a long time since anyone had called Hawk young, but Gail was her same age, so it was probably just wishful thinking. "Maybe. But a man with the amount of shrapnel I've got in me would have a corner office at the Pentagon."

"One of your men... Forest, I think, said something about medals. Afghanistan?"

"And Iraq. And one I can't talk about." Hawk looked up and their eyes met. She was used to civilians' pity when she talked about her service, but it was unpleasant to see it on such a beautiful face. She cleared her throat and her voice was ice when she changed the subject. "So you think Drumm is going to be a problem?"

Gail handled the shift well, though a flash of confusion crossed her face so quickly Hawk might have imagined it. "Yes, I do. He has been advocating for what he calls a clean sweep." She put her glass down and leaned forward, her elbows resting against the white tablecloth. "I think I should make it known that I am firm on wanting a nonviolent conclusion."

"It's my hope that a show of force will be enough to make them back down. There is a very big difference between taking on a dozen glorified mall cops and taking on an entire Special Forces company. I intend to do everything in my power to avoid bloodshed."

"I'm happy to hear that."

"Are you? It wouldn't be cheap for Andrus to have to send up a whole new batch of workers, I suppose."

Whether it was the insinuation or the ironic inflection she had placed on the word "workers," blood flooded Gail's earlobes and neck. She stood so quickly that the glass tipped and spun on its wide base. They both watched it for a moment, wondering if it would fall. It righted itself with a melodic whine of crystal, and she turned to the door, saying over her shoulder to Hawk, "If you are finished with your dinner, we shouldn't keep Derek waiting."

CHAPTER NINE

By the time Hawk arrived with Gail at the security team's staging area, two Charlie Company platoons were already there, to the visible relief of the civilian guards being sent out of harm's way. They gathered near the exit like a flock of spooked sheep, trembling to get out of danger. The only person in street clothes who looked in the least bit upset to be leaving was a large man who was shouting at one of her officers.

"I'm guessing that would be Derek Drumm?"

"In the flesh." Gail frowned as he spotted them and came storming in their direction. "Be careful, it seems he's in a mood."

As he charged over, Hawk had the chance to take the measure of the man. He was about her height, but with more than his share of stomach. He had the powerful build of a person who was used to years of hard work, but his abdomen proved those years had long since passed. His belly strained against the buttons of his black uniform shirt and sagged to the bottom of his wide leather belt. Attached to the belt was a pistol in a holster of shiny, pristine leather. It would be a miracle if he could even remove the weapon from its stiff casing should the occasion ever arise. His hair was fading to an insubstantial gray at his temples, and his eyes were buried between a heavy forehead and round, red cheeks. He possessed the weakest chin that Hawk had ever seen and his large Adam's apple bobbed in his fleshy neck when he arrived shouting at Gail.

"You wanna tell me why no one bothered to inform me that the Army was here to Monday-morning quarterback my operation? They're trying to kick me and my men out of my own station!"

Hawk took a step forward, positioning herself subtly between Gail and the sweating man. "To call us Monday-morning quarterbacks would imply that the operation is over, which I'm sure you can see it is not." Now that she had his attention, she shifted her voice to a more neutral tone and continued, "Major Charlie Hawk, US Army Special Forces. You must be Derek Drumm. Pleased to meet you."

"*Captain* Drumm."

Hawk had no intention of using the title. It was one that meant something to her. In her world brave men and women fought and bled to earn it, but he had bestowed the honor upon himself merely to stroke his ego and because he led a group of men. Still, it wouldn't help to be antagonistic.

She gave him a tight nod and said, "Thank you for keeping everything calm and secure, Drumm." She turned to Gail and hid her conspiratorial wink from him. "Could you help my men with the diagrams of this wing while we discuss the situation? They're used to military engineer designs, and I'd hate for us to bust a water pipe because we're reading it wrong."

Gail smiled politely at Hawk, moving off toward a small knot of officers huddled around a metal table. Hawk took a steadying breath and turned back to the security guard. "Now that the civilians are out of the way, perhaps you could give me some advice on the situation here before you and your men fall back to protect the housing block?"

He was pathetically easy to manipulate. He had preened openly at her scant praise earlier, and now he was clearly pleased that he had been asked for his expert opinion. The fact that she had maneuvered him into retreating hadn't seemed to register, and she hoped to keep it that way.

Drumm crossed his arms and said, "You want my advice? Forget what the suits have to say. You gas 'em. That's what you do. There are doors with airtight seals at the end of every corridor in this facility. You shut the one on this side. You shut the one on the other side. Then you send someone out in the space suits they use for mining and you open one of the emergency airlocks." He made a gesture like sweeping papers off a desk. "Suck 'em out into space and you won't even have to clean up the bodies. Get a whole new crop of skinhead murderers and kiddie rapists up here. This time you shackle their ankles like a chain gang. Take away their satellite TV. Take away their cake three times a week. Take away their books and their days off and all the other perks that bleeding-heart dyke in charge here insists on them having. They'll be scared already because they'll know what we did to this lot of assholes and they'll keep in line."

With every word, the sour taste of bile rose in the back of Hawk's throat, but she schooled herself to keep her disgust hidden. He licked his lips to collect the frothy white specks at the corners and rubbed a hand across the red splotches on his neck and ears.

Hawk held out her hand toward him as she spoke, "Thank you for the insight." He squeezed unnecessarily hard and shook it too vigorously. "I have a squad assigned to protect the civilian housing block, but they don't know this place or these people like you do. If you would take your men to the main courtyard and supplement their patrols, I'm sure it would ease the minds of the corporate folks."

"Bunch of pansies that don't have any business here." He sighed and rolled his eyes, but he moved off to gather his men.

She watched his men hustle from the room with more initiative than she had seen from them as yet. Drumm was the last through the door, shouting insults at the men at the rear who were moving too slowly for his taste.

Hawk shook her head and said in a low voice, "Charming."

"Isn't he?" She turned to see that Gail had returned to her side, looking far more comfortable away from Drumm. "I've had to deal with him for three damn years. You worked him quite efficiently. Well done."

Hawk tried not to be too pleased with the praise. "Thank you. I've unfortunately had a lot of practice with his type. They aren't all quite so sweaty though."

Gail laughed, a rich sound that felt like a warm day. Hawk found herself wondering if Drumm was telling the truth when he called her a dyke or if he was just using it as an insult.

As the quick spout of laughter faded away, Gail's face sobered. "So what was his advice?"

"Seal off the corridor, open the air locks, and start with a new bunch of convicts in leg irons."

Gail paled visibly and Hawk suddenly felt guilty about her insinuation at dinner. It was clear she didn't see the prisoners as assets rather than people.

"I hope that isn't an option that you are seriously considering, because I…"

Hawk held up a hand to cut her off. "Absolutely not. I consider that the last resort."

Some of the tension fell out of her shoulders. "Thank you, Major. These men were brought here due to an overwhelming public objection to capital punishment. One that I share, incidentally. To treat them as disposable now would be contrary to the country's attitudes."

"I can't rule out anything yet, but I'd like to try negotiation first. Is there some way to communicate with the prisoners?"

Gail motioned to a panel on the wall. "We have an internal communications network with a phone and loudspeaker in every room and corridor. Mostly they're for emergencies. There's a panel in the mess hall. I could try putting a call through."

"Please."

* * *

"The answer is no."

"I have every right to be there."

"You certainly do, but it is not going to happen. This is a military operation now and I cannot risk civilian safety or interference. I don't know what I'm dealing with yet. Until I do, it's not safe for you to be there."

"Then give me a bulletproof vest. Those men are my responsibility."

"No, they aren't." Captain Williams had been hovering just out of earshot, holding Hawk's gear and already decked in his tactical armor and helmet. Hawk waved him over as she continued, "The moment you called in the United States Army, they became my responsibility. As did you, and I won't put you in harm's way without cause."

Gail crossed her arms. Her scowl hollowed her thin cheeks as she watched the major strap a vest over her uniform. "That's unfair."

"No, it isn't fair. It's reality." Hawk shook her head at the helmet Williams held out to her and strapped her sidearm into place. "More importantly, the prisoners most likely see you as the embodiment of the corporation they're rebelling against. You're the figurehead. I'm trying to negotiate a peaceful surrender, and I can't do that if I bring their enemy to the meeting. I'll be wearing a body camera and mic, so you can watch and listen. Your impressions will be helpful when I get back. I need you here."

Williams held out the helmet again. "Major, it is standard protocol to…"

"That will be all, Captain."

He used his crisp salute and heel turn to communicate his disagreement, and Gail's cold stare was no less expressive. As Williams moved to join a pair of officers in full battle gear standing by the makeshift barricade at the end of the hall, Gail spoke up, "I'm much smarter than my Head of Security, Major Hawk. I know when I'm being handled."

"You aren't being handled, Ms. Moore. You're being protected." Gail's eyes flashed with anger, looking like twin blocks of amber in the clinical lighting. "Look, you know this facility and these people better than I do, better than any of my men do. I would appreciate your advice if you are willing to give it."

Hawk had hoped that the softening of her tone would have some effect, but it seemed only to offend her more. She might have found a kindred spirit in this woman who was confident and used to being in charge, but those attributes were unhelpful at the moment. When it became clear Hawk wouldn't change her mind, Gail stormed off in the direction of a large table laden with an array of electronic equipment.

Watching her go led Hawk's eyes to a small cluster of people standing by the table. They were shifting in that way that could either indicate anxiety or excitement. People who had no idea what to expect next. Their behavior was familiar to her from that of reporters in a war zone. Sure enough, as she scanned the faces, she recognized Stone, the man she met on the plane. Oddly, he was the only one who appeared perfectly at ease, his eyes fixed on her and the wide, empty grin still on his face.

She started off down the hallway toward her team. She stopped a few paces away from them to recheck her gear and collect her thoughts. Behind them was the prisoners' barricade, a cobbled-together pile of furniture and assorted garbage. It filled a section of the long corridor between the two cafeterias from floor to ceiling just behind an abandoned security gate. As she watched, someone on the other side shifted a metal bookshelf, opening a small gap. Just like she always did before entering an active zone, Hawk tapped the first two fingers of her left hand to the American flag patch on her shoulder. Then she marched on, past the team of men that fell into formation at her heels.

CHAPTER TEN

Gail studiously ignored the sound of retreating steps as Hawk marched out of the room. It took a great deal of self-control not to turn and watch the soldiers go. Instead, she continued her own walk to the big table buzzing with uniformed men and machines. A figure detached from the group as she approached and she thought he intended to stop her. Gail was fully prepared to unload her considerable anger when she recognized him. A wide smile broke across his boyish face and he held out a hand to her.

"Captain Forest, Logistics. We met in the hangar."

"Of course, Captain." Years in the corporate world had given Gail plenty of practice at pretending to remember names, but she wasn't entirely sure she fooled this particular man. "Major Hawk asked me to assist."

"To be honest, I wasn't sure she'd win that little battle, Administrator. I'm not sure she was prepared for another woman as stubborn as she is."

Despite her best efforts, she couldn't quite bring herself to think less of him for his comment. He had that assertive familiarity she disliked so much in some men, but there was a genuineness to him as well. She was suddenly reminded that this man was fully prepared to die here, far away from his friends and family on Earth, to save her life. It was a powerful reminder of his character, so she ignored his conceit.

"Captain Forest?" A female African-American soldier called from the table. "She's in."

Gail followed Forest over to the table. He pulled up a pair of folding chairs to a flat-screen monitor and handed her a headset. She ignored the chair and settled the single headphone over her right ear. The audio was remarkably clear. Listening closely, Gail could hear soft, rhythmic breathing and concluded that it was Major Hawk's since her name appeared at the bottom of the video feed playing on the monitor.

"High-def body cams," Forest explained. "Hell of a lot better than the ones cops back home wear."

"How would you know?" The female soldier called quietly from the monitor next to them. "It's not like they turn theirs on."

Forest responded in his usual joking tone, but Gail tuned them out, focusing on the video image in front of her. Hawk paused as she entered the prisoners' cafeteria and looked around, shifting her body slowly and carefully, allowing those watching to see a full range of the scene before her. Both the soldiers immediately started scribbling notes and consulting with each other, noting the position of objects and people in the camera's somewhat wobbly view.

Gail never ate in the cafeteria, let alone the prisoners' cafeteria. Her meals were either taken in the little kitchenette in her apartment or in the executive dining room on the top floor. Like the rest of Moon Base, however, she toured it regularly. The last time she'd inspected the cafeteria was early this month, long before the troubles began. She'd been through it close to midnight, when the prisoners were all locked down in their rooms and the stoves and ovens were cold. Everything had been neat and orderly then. It had looked nothing like this.

"It's like *West Side Story* meets *Mad Max*," Forest said, his conversation ended and his focus back on the screen.

Gail noticed the guns first. She'd watched the takeover footage often enough to know the prisoners breached the weapons cache located in a corridor linking the farming pod to the main structure, but the extent of their armament was now shockingly clear. With their chins thrown up and the gleam of power in their eyes, only about one in ten of the fifty men carried assault rifles, but it was enough. Those that were armed looked like they were ten feet tall.

Oddly, Gail had seen few weapons among the soldiers. She hadn't thought about it until now. The officers she'd met, including Major Hawk, all wore handguns on their hips and the four men who accompanied her into the cafeteria all had rifles, but the soldiers left behind with her and Forest seemed unarmed. In fact, her own security force seemed to be far more heavily armed in their day-to-day routine.

It wasn't just the guns that were out of place. Most of the furniture was gone, presumably used in the creation of the barricade. In their place, mattresses had been strewn across the floor in some places, discarded clothing and food wrappers in others. Books and magazines, normally restricted to the library or prisoner rooms, were hanging open on the floor. Sofas Gail recognized from the prisoner rec room were here as well, stains from dirty boots and food splattered on every cushion. It seemed they had all moved into this one room since erecting the barricade.

Groups of men sat on particle-board tables with attached stools or lounged against the painted concrete walls. Some were young with bulging muscles, some middle-aged with sagging jowls. All of the faces were familiar to Gail, even if she could only remember a fraction of their names. Despite her best efforts to know the prisoners, her daily work was far removed from theirs. The gulf between the two populations of Moon Base had never felt so wide.

Many of the men were shirtless, showing off tattooed chests. Most looked like they could use a shower. Gail was no warden, that role was purposefully absent here, Andrus preferring to run the colony as a business venture rather than a prison. Drumm and his men handled the security of the prisoners, but Gail was in charge of everyone here and she insisted on a certain level of decorum. That was what separated Moon Base from an Earth prison. The idea was to give the men the dignity not found in the yard at a high-security prison. She'd assumed they felt respected. Felt like more than rats in a cage because she treated them like employees rather than a chain gang. Obviously not.

The camera shifted slightly as Hawk crossed the cafeteria. On the GPS map superimposed on the upper corner of the video display, the cluster of red dots that represented the members of the team fanned out. Hawk walked at the front of an arrow-point formation, a pair of soldiers flanking her on either side. Gail knew the other soldiers were armed, but she still held her breath as the little group moved through the crowd. There were only five of them to the fifty prisoners, but they moved with authority. They marched in time and some of the older prisoners looked somewhat cowed. The younger men visible in the camera frame, mostly those covered in gang tattoos, tried to look menacing, but only managed to look foolish. The armed prisoners looked cautiously neutral. At least their leader had made sure to put weapons only in sure hands. Gail felt some comfort in that.

Some of the tables had been folded up and pushed against the wall, for all the world like a deserted middle-school cafeteria, leaving a wide open space at the center of the room. The prisoners backed away, clearing a walkway down the center of the room, leading to a table with a much larger cluster of men around it.

Gail watched as Hawk traveled the gauntlet. It was an impressive sight. She could feel the strength of the soldiers in the cadence of their boots ringing off the polished linoleum floor as it echoed through the crystal-clear audio connection.

In her introductory phone call with the prisoners, Hawk had announced her identity and the presence of her team here on Moon Base, and if they had contemplated fighting, the Army's display of might would resonate with them. Gail found herself impressed with Major Hawk, despite their prickly encounters. The woman knew how to make an entrance.

"Time for the show," Forest said in a low voice, his eyes locked on the screen.

A show. If that's what this was, Gail was fine with it. She needed to see the face of the man in charge of the insurrection. She knew who he was. He hadn't tried to hide his identity, even at the start. What she wanted was to look into her enemy's eyes. She would know his intentions then.

As they approached the main group men looked up at them and slithered away. They retreated to the walls and whispered or melted into the back of the surrounding crowd. Not until the huddle had broken up was Gail aware of the man at the center of it. He was visible now, sitting easily on the table top, his feet on a pair of stools in front of him, elbows on knees. He wore a wide grin, showing bright white teeth between a thin, well-trimmed mustache and goatee liberally streaked with silver. His eyes sparkled with mischief and his jaw was square and broad. A pair of hard-faced men stood on either side of him, cradling their weapons awkwardly. Hawk stopped in front of the leader and waited for him to speak, testing to see if the silence would unnerve him. Gail knew it would not.

His smile didn't falter an inch, but he was the one who broke the stalemate. "Good evening. Welcome to Moon Base. I would offer you a drink like a good host, but alcohol is one of the many luxuries we are denied here."

"Thank you for the welcome." Hawk spread her gaze evenly among all the men, being sure to turn her body slightly as she did to give the camera a wide sweep. "I'm Charlie Hawk, United States Army."

"No need to be coy, Major Hawk. I see the Special Forces insignia. What are you, 3SFGA? You can call me Red. No rank or anything, just Red's fine."

Gail had no idea what 3SFGA was, but, based on the way Forest's neck snapped to share a look with the female soldier, Red shouldn't have known either.

Hawk didn't miss a beat. "Are you an Army man, Red?"

He dropped a foot to the floor, exposing a dusty work boot under his prison jeans. Gail made a mental note to tell Hawk that Red worked in the agricultural pod rather than the mining operation, hence the dirt.

"For a bit and a piece. Stationed at Bragg for a little while before I was mobilized to Iraq. Not the good one, mind. Too old for that. The pussy one back in the Nineties. Desert Storm. What a joke. Desert Vacation more like."

"I'm not sure I would call the second Iraq War 'the good one.' At least not from my experience of it."

A look of concern spread over his face. "I'm sorry, ma'am. That was disrespectful of me. No intention to offend, I assure you."

Knowing the man, Gail was certain he had, in fact, meant to offend. He wanted to see if he could get a rise out of Hawk and he had.

Forest turned accusing eyes on her. "You didn't say he was ex-military."

"I wasn't aware it was relevant."

"Everything is relevant when we're in theatre, ma'am."

Gail sighed, turning from the screen reluctantly. "I have an obligation to protect the privacy of my staff."

"He ain't staff. He's a prisoner."

"He is a resident of my facility and I have limited access to his prison records because it is my responsibility to treat him with the same dignity as my civilian staff. I am certainly not at liberty to share them."

"Well, all due respect ma'am, you want to live through this, you might wanna share that one record."

Gail turned back to the screen. "I'll take that under advisement."

"I wasn't much of a soldier, if I'm bein' honest," Red was saying, his winning smile back in place. "Got into a few fights and none of them on the battlefield. I had a wild youth. Scrubbed out in ninety-three when they'd had just about enough of me. Anyway, we have more important things to discuss than my dubious history in this man's Army."

"That's true, we do," Hawk responded, a lightness to her voice that Gail was not expecting. "What can you tell me about what's going on here, Red?"

"You mean the powers that be haven't filled you in?"

His tone was skeptical but pleasant and Hawk matched it perfectly. "Of course they did, but I'd like to hear your version."

"You don't trust what the suits told you."

It wasn't a question and Gail bristled at the thought he might be right.

"I think there's always at least two sides to every story. I'd like to avoid a confrontation if I can, but it doesn't look too good for you at the moment. I'm hoping there's something you can tell me that will make all this make sense."

He laughed, a loud, barking guffaw not unlike the one that he gave when Gail went to visit him at the first signs of a problem. It made her skin crawl that day and it made her skin crawl now.

"I like you, Major." He laughed again, this time for so long that some of the men around him shifted nervously, looking at each other. "I like you, but you can't bullshit me. You say you don't want a confrontation, but you bring your boys in here with more than just their dicks in their hands. You think I'm supposed to trust that?"

The camera stood perfectly still, not even moving with Hawk's breathing, and her voice was ice-covered stone. "It's a little rich for you to be indignant about my men carrying weapons when your men are openly armed. Why don't we just stop the posturing and get to business."

One of his bodyguards stepped forward, his lip curling as he stared up at her, but Red put out a hand and grabbed his forearm. He stopped, but he did not retreat and Red nodded.

"Okay. I'm a reasonable man, after all. Where should I start?"

"How about you start with what happened to kick off all of this and move on to what you want?"

"There was no straw that broke the camel's back, if that's what you're asking. Just a steady stream of injustice and lies that became intolerable for us." He rubbed his palms together, warming to his chance to speak, as Gail knew he would. She wondered how Hawk had known. "We are none of us saints. We've all admitted our crimes and asked the Lord for his forgiveness. We know we have to atone in this life for deliverance in the next, and we accepted the price we were quoted."

As he stood up and moved around the room, looking to the faces of the men around him as he told their story, Gail felt herself being drawn in. It was compelling, the way he spoke of God and forgiveness. Except that Gail knew he was not a member of any church and had been vocal about his atheism for many years. Over the years he had told her some of his crimes, usually in the manner of a remorseful confession, and they were heinous. They were the actions of a man who believed in nothing, especially the very church he had evoked, but she also saw the way some of the men around him, particularly the older ones, seemed to stand taller when he spoke.

"They brought us here before there was a here. Just inflatable tents and piles of construction materials, the scent of sweat and death constantly in the air. I was in that group of early settlers. Many of these men were here as well. We poured the foundations and raised the walls and we earned our adventure with hard work."

He raised his arms to the ceiling like a minister at a tent revival. Gail wanted to argue, but she hadn't been here in those days. She had come, like most of the current civilian workers, after these men had built their own prison.

"This magnificent structure you see today was made with these hands before you. We even raised the bars that we knew would restrain us. We did it all willingly because promises were made, but they have not been kept."

"Tell me about the promises." Hawk's voice cut in, breaking his cadence and earning a scowl.

The camera followed Red as he crossed the room, squeezing the shoulder of a young man with wet eyes and a hang-dog look.

"We were told that our lives would be freer here. That we could move around the complex and do what we wanted while we weren't working. Then they decided they would need corporate people up here, so we were sequestered to half the main structure. Even there we have strict curfews and our rooms are constantly searched.

"We do all the work around here. Farming, tending the livestock, loading and unloading the planes, even down to the laundry. Meanwhile the white collars sit in their pretty offices and count the money we're making for them. We do everything and we can't so much as take a piss without someone watching."

"Were there written promises or were these just your expectations?" Hawk asked. "I've seen the contracts for secured personnel. Apart from clemency on death sentences, there was nothing about earning freedom that I saw."

"You know corporate types never put anything in writing."

"Is that so?" There was a smile in Hawk's voice no doubt caused by the petulance of his last remark. "I'm career military, Red. I don't know how businesses operate."

"They operate on the backs of hardworking men like us." Red gave a sweeping gesture to the men around him and there was a general grumble of ascent. Hawk's attempt to talk him into a corner had failed, and he was back to the benevolent preacher, pontificating to his flock. He kept moving around the room, looking at the other prisoners rather than Hawk.

"They told us our families could come visit, but the only flights they can take are on the shipping runs. They say space is at a premium and they charge ridiculous rates for each seat. None of us have anyone that can afford the trip. They can't send packages over a certain weight. During the dark days they can't even call us. We had more contact when we were behind bars on Earth."

"Surely that doesn't surprise you, Red. You're not on the same planet."

"A man can't live without his family, Major." He turned stone eyes on her, but Gail felt the rebuke herself. "He starts to lose everything when he can't see his mother's face. You have to understand that."

Frustration of not being present for this meeting started to nag at Gail. She felt herself start to sweat. Something felt wrong.

"I understand. What else?"

"A man has needs, Major." He gave her a searching look from head to toe, a smirk on his weathered face. "I have a feeling you know what I'm talking about even though, as a Southern gentleman, I can't spell it out. Don't Ask, Don't Tell must have had the same effect for you, am I right? Here you are, Special Forces, Green Beret. That's guaranteed to drop the panties of half the ladies in the bar, but the Army tells you no. We're astronauts! We do space walks and live on the Moon! Those jackass security guards parlay that into a heap of tail when they get home and we're stuck here with nothing. It's cruel and unusual."

Gail forced herself to breathe steadily. She knew what was wrong now, though Forest only seemed to notice the reference to Hawk's sexuality. He shared a look with the female soldier when Red had mentioned the Army's stance on homosexuality, but Gail heard the real implications. Red was demanding something he could not have. What did he expect her to do? Set up a brothel for the prisoners?

"We work six days a week here. If we're on mining rotations, we go to the asteroid belt to haul back those rocks and work day in and day out for three-week stretches. The weightlessness does a number on our bones. Those of us who were on the first crew can't go into space anymore. We work on the farm and tend the livestock that feed the prisoners and the white collars alike. We do the mining, we do the farming, we do the loading at The Docks. We do everything and they reap the rewards." He turned back to Hawk, his jaw set. "That needs to change."

"And how would you like to see things change?"

He strolled back to the table, content that every eye was on him. He preened and crossed his arms across his chest. "I reckon they'll have to go."

"Who will have to go?"

"The white collars." He let that statement completely fade to silence before starting again. Gail was familiar with his showmanship and, for the stillness of her voice, Major Hawk seemed to be taking it in stride. "Are you a student of history? Do you know the history of British colonies?"

"Why don't you tell me?"

"Take Australia. It started an awful lot like Moon Base. A prison colony full of the worst offenders that England had to offer. The Limeys sent 'em off on a boat to the other side of the world and kept 'em in chains and made 'em build a whole new country while the company men, the soldiers, did nothing but get fat off the prisoners' work. No contact with their loved ones, nowhere to run, nothing but their old lives. But they built a new life and because they built it, it was theirs. They served out their time and they got to go free. Got their rights back and made their own lives. America wasn't too different. Some of us were prisoners, too. Not all pilgrims and explorers. When we got free of the British, we decided America was our home and we wanted to keep it. Maybe if the Aussie watched us close enough they'd have done the same once they got their pardons. I expect we've worked hard enough up here in our colony, time for us to do like our boy Washington. That's my offer."

The abrupt shift from lecture to demand caught Gail off guard, but not Hawk.

"You know that isn't an offer, Red. It's a threat and it will be met with the sort of response that threats are usually met with."

Red stood and stepped forward. Gail flinched, but the camera didn't. She recognized the movement for what it was, a carefully calculated aggression. Not enough to get shot over, but not enough to be ignored either.

"There is only one option. I suggest you remove the civilians for their own safety. Put them on a plane and follow them to your own seats. Pull up stakes and leave us be." He shifted his eyes to stare directly into the camera on her shoulder. Directly into Gail's eyes. "Leave that pretty little CEO and those two secretaries she's got and we'll even let you take the last of the goods we mined."

He knew Gail was watching. He wasn't talking to Hawk—
he was talking to her. Ice flooded through Gail and her vision
tightened to a pinprick at the end of a tunnel. It wasn't the first
time she'd been threatened by a prisoner here, though most of
them were surprisingly docile. It was, however, the first time she
had heard someone barter a few metric tons of raw platinum in
exchange for her unwilling body. Gail found it an unpleasant
experience.

While Gail was stoic, Hawk snapped. There was a rustling
noise and the camera shot disappeared in a jumble of fabric.
She'd charged forward, closing the gap between them to inches.

Her voice came out through clenched teeth as a muffled
growl. "It is inadvisable for you to threaten the safety of people
under my protection."

There was a rattle of movement. Gail thought she heard the
distinct metallic noise of weapons being readied. Forest started
talking low and fast into his headset. She heard the sound of
running feet.

It all cut off abruptly as Red's voice, pitched low and
completely without the thick North Carolina accent, came
through. "It's no threat. You think those women haven't come
to me already?" His normal volume and cadence reappeared.
"You have twelve hours until we cross the dark horizon, Major.
Things swing in our favor when that happens. Make your
decision quickly. I have the utmost respect for our military, but
I will kill anyone who tries to take what's mine."

Hawk stepped back and Red's grinning face came back into
view.

"You know they feel the same way, right? Andrus still sees
this place as theirs and they're going to fight for it. Why do you
think I'm here?"

"Then I guess you're going to war again, Major Hawk."

CHAPTER ELEVEN

The Docks were alive with activity. Hawk's soldiers moved with well-practiced purpose. Hawk watched them from her Command Center in the hangar and felt instantly at ease. No matter where she was in the universe or what she was up against, her people were the best of the best and that was enough for her.

What Hawk didn't like was the tent around her. Not long ago the military in its infinite wisdom had switched to a new tent style. They had a modern design that was actually very similar to the structure of the Moon Base dome, with a spherical internal support of overlapping triangles covered in nylon tarp. The result was a rounded, oblong shape that the Pentagon claimed was more conducive to the sort of harsh environments a military unit might experience. Like everything else from the new military contractors, the nylon was cheap and smelled like burnt motor oil. The ceilings were too low and the tent itself, billed as a simple setup, was an ungainly beast both collapsed and fully expanded. Still, Hawk had to admit they served their purpose.

Beyond this tent there was a forest of smaller ones dotting the hangar's stained concrete floor. Most were for sleeping, with bunks stacked into every inch. Others were for mess, infirmary, supplies and command. In a few short hours this empty hangar had become a functioning military camp able to support her full company for the duration. Apart from clean water, they needed nothing from Moon Base.

Master Sergeant Benton moved through the crowd like the only adult on a playground. He'd served with Hawk for too many years for her to recall, but his face remembered every one of them. It was lined in a million places, but he was still quick with a smile no matter what the mission. Despite his years or perhaps because of them, his broad shoulders towered over the other soldiers and his hair, now mostly gray, was a beacon that drew every eye.

"Major," he said, snapping to attention and sliding into a perfectly formed salute. "Ready to report, ma'am."

She returned the salute and ushered him into the tent. Williams poured over maps and Forest rewatched the video. Benton refused a seat at the table. She would have insisted if she thought it would do any good. He looked dead on his feet.

"How was your meeting with Mr. Drumm?"

Benton was too good a soldier to make any outward display of annoyance in front of his commander. Instead, he held his rigid pose, chin high and chest thrown out, and replied, "He's a wannabe, but I can handle him, ma'am."

"A wannabe?" Forest barked, turning his head away from the monitor to laugh. "That's some pretty old slang."

Benton did not shift his pose a muscle, even to look over at Forest laughing at him. "I'm pretty old, sir. What of it?"

Forest's laughter died in his throat and his expression melted into confusion. Instead of replying, he turned back to the monitor, ostentatiously scribbling a note. A whisper of a smile curled on Benton's lips but disappeared just as quickly as it arrived.

"I've instituted a roster of patrols in the civilian living

quarters," Benton said, swallowing a yawn with moderate success as he spoke. "We're doing our best to interact with the locals, ma'am, but they're pretty freaked out. Keeping to their rooms."

"That's good news," Hawk replied, pacing the tent and trying to calculate the hours her team had been awake. "Keep the civilians out of the equation as much as possible."

"That's the idea, ma'am."

"Your team is interfacing with the security force?"

"Yes, ma'am. I've set up a patrol schedule that pairs one of ours with one of theirs. I think the civilians are less frightened now that they see us there."

"Thank you, Master Sergeant. Now go hit the sack."

He was less successful at hiding the second yawn. It pulled down on his face, making the skin appear even more leathery than usual. "Not quite yet, ma'am. I need to meet with a few more of the men. Discuss protocol."

"We'll handle it. Get some sleep."

"Ma'am..."

"That's an order, Master Sergeant Benton."

His whole body stiffened as he snapped into another perfect salute. "Ma'am. Yes, ma'am."

She dismissed him and turned her attention back to her clipboard. Her quick movements allowed her to catch the middle finger Forest shot Benton with a smile and a wink. She didn't see him return it, but she knew enough about her staff to know that he did. When Benton's footsteps receded out of earshot she spoke, her eyes still on the list in front of her.

"Is there *any* soldier in Charlie Company with whom you maintain a professional relationship, Captain Forest?"

"Not that I'm aware of, ma'am."

Williams responded with laughter in his voice, "At least he's consistent."

Hawk ignored them both, trying hard not to be too annoyed with them. This was just how they worked. Everyone handled stress in their own way, and it wasn't always her way. The strain on her tense shoulders and the fatigue in her jaw from clenching her teeth all day were evidence that she might do well to take a page from Forest's book. Williams told her constantly that she needed to relax, but that simply wasn't an option for her. She was too old a dog to learn new tricks.

"Private," she called out to one of her support staff setting up a surveillance system in the corner of the tent. He sprang to his feet and stood in front of her so quickly that he must've been waiting for new orders. "Round up the guards assigned to the civilian living quarters to clarify their security protocols."

He saluted and slipped past her to the mouth of the tent almost before the words were out of her mouth.

"While you're at it, please make sure the sentries understand their routes." Hawk handed him the patrol map from her clipboard. Earlier in the day she'd sketched it out, marking each access point to the power station and each control room that could be used to remotely access the power grid. "I don't want anyone moving in this facility without us knowing about it."

The private left with the map, moving smoothly around another soldier entering the tent. The new soldier left just as quickly, barely stopping to hand a sheet of paper to Williams before returning to her post. Hawk watched her go, taking note of how sure-footed and clear-eyed she was. At least some members of her team had rested.

Hawk made a note on her clipboard to institute a sleep rotation as soon as possible. Her list, written in her small, block script on several sheets of graph paper, was one hundred twenty-two entries long. She crossed out the line establishing sentry routes in high-risk areas, but that one accomplishment did little to improve her mood. There was far too much to do.

"Bad news, Major," Williams said, still scanning the message. "We've been unable to reach the hostiles on the base phone lines. Looks like negotiations are officially over."

The news didn't surprise Hawk. Red didn't strike her as the sort of man who would compromise. He didn't even strike her as the kind of man who would talk, unless it was to stroke his own ego or show off in front of his men. No, she hadn't expected further communication so soon, but it was still disappointing. They were getting dangerously close to the dark horizon and they still had no options for a peaceful resolution. She hadn't felt this powerless since Afghanistan, and she didn't relish an outcome like that.

"Damn," she said, transferring her attention from the long list to the tactical map Williams had been examining. "I was really hoping for another chance."

"You can't be too surprised," Forest said, switching off his monitor and coming over to join them at the table. "That guy was a real hard ass."

The three of them looked over the map in silence for a long time. It was crude, more of a basic floorplan than an architectural drawing. One of the many issues with a mission thrown together at such short notice was the lack of hard data. She'd asked for blueprints of the base, but the structure was massive and the plans were hard to come by. Hawk hadn't seen them yet.

Taped to the table beside the floorplan was a sheet of paper, written in many hands, with strategy options. Hawk had seen technology, particularly the unproven technology tested in military actions, fail more times than she was comfortable with. She liked to work the old-fashioned way. Power outages didn't matter when you worked with pencil and paper. Her officers, particularly Forest, adapted to her style out of necessity but they were rarely happy about it. They wanted their tablets and their laptops. She wanted something she could hold, only breaking out her laptop when she was forced.

Williams clearly noticed her focus shift to the list because he immediately started discussing the contents. "Our nonviolent options are slim, Major."

"They're also the only ones I'm considering at this stage."

Forest brought up his favorite option first. "Take them by surprise. Go in when they're sleeping and secure the weapons before they can fight back."

"Too risky," Hawk replied immediately. "They've blocked the security cameras so we can't know when they're sleeping. It would be monumentally stupid not to keep a watch. There's fifty of them, so they could have a very effective roster. Red said he's ex-military. He won't make that mistake. There would be heavy casualties."

"Have we confirmed his claims?" Williams asked.

"Not yet," Forest answered. "Andrus corporate has refused us access to prison records and Ms. Moore says they've forbidden her from turning it over. All information is currently on lockdown."

Hawk waved a dismissive hand. "Doesn't matter whether he's lying or not. It isn't worth the risk."

"Lock down the cafeteria. Cut them off from the rest of the facility and wait for them to surrender," Williams suggested.

"It's unlikely they're all in the cafeteria even though they seem to be nesting there. They'll be taking trips to showers and collecting food from the other domes. Someone on the outside could let them out with access to a security computer terminal. Besides, they have access to way too much food and water to make that a logical option."

Hawk nodded along at Forest's counterpoint, letting the arguments ripple through the stillness of her mind like wind across the surface of a lake. The answer was out there, they just had to find it, and this workshopping was the best way to figure it out. Her shoulders relaxed just talking about the problem.

"Send in different communication devices." Forest turned back to his electronics equipment and grabbed a heavy phone that looked like an old walky-talky. "Send in our own comms on a field robot and open up talks again."

Hawk responded to this one. "The base phones work just fine, they just aren't answering. Sending in another phone for them to ignore won't help our situation. He won't talk."

She had seen Red's look when their conversation ended last time. He had a gleam in his eye when he talked about Administrator Moore Hawk didn't like. His insinuation made her want to scream. As though she would leave that beautiful woman alone on this dead rock at the whim of a man like that. Hawk's pulse pounded in her neck and she knew she was losing focus. Still, she couldn't help but revel in the burning anger inside her for just a moment.

If she really examined their situation, Hawk knew there was little chance of a peaceful resolution. More than that, if she really examined her own heart right now, she didn't want to fight that hard to save a man like Red. A man who could think of a woman, any woman, but especially one like Administrator Moore as though she were a piece of meat wasn't worth saving.

That was the real problem, of course, and Hawk knew it. She wanted to protect the civilians, but there was a special need to protect Gail. A need that had nothing to do with the pips on her sleeve and everything to do with the way Hawk's pulse quickened at the sight of her. It'd been a long time since anyone affected Hawk as this woman did, and she wasn't quite ready, or able, to give up that distraction.

"Keep working on it. I'm not killing those men if I don't have to," Hawk said, being sure to speak in plurals.

"Even Red?"

She shot Williams a look, noticing that he wasn't fooled by her attempt at covering her emotions. She didn't risk answering him though. Her instinct to protect a beautiful woman should not be enough to take a man's life. Still, the choice may not be hers to make.

"Just keep looking."

CHAPTER TWELVE

Gail didn't bother to look up at the chirp from her monitor. It had chirped the same way for the last fifteen minutes and displayed the same message. *Please hold the line while your party connects.* She'd been holding the line, but her party didn't seem that eager to connect. It really wasn't too much of an inconvenience. She had plenty of paperwork, even during this crisis.

After another dozen pages and another three signatures, the tone of the chirp changed and Gail pushed her papers aside. What she saw made her scowl for a heartbeat before schooling her features. It wouldn't do for Andrus CEO Walter Compton to hear about her bad attitude. He wouldn't see it himself because, despite his assurances about the importance of this call, it was not Walter's face materializing before her.

Michael Richards was the sort of man who called himself "Assistant to the CEO Walter Compton" even when Walter referred to him as his secretary. He was young, but not as young as he made himself appear. He took pains to keep his cheeks smooth and soft and his nails perfectly manicured. His ties were always a bold splash of color on an otherwise professionally bland outfit, but that wasn't what unfailingly drew Gail's eye. The sleeves of all his suits were just an inch too long and she found it wildly distracting. In her estimation, this touch of sloppiness conveyed a lack of attention to detail that was unforgivable in their line of work. If he couldn't buy a suit jacket that fit properly, he had no business working in the CEO's office.

"Good evening, Ms. Moore. Or is it morning there? I can never remember."

Gail gritted her teeth through her smile. "It's evening here, Michael. We go by New York time here to be consistent with the corporate office."

"Oh yes, of course." He had the aggressive habit of looking directly into the camera as though he were trying to stare her down. Normally Gail took it in her stride, but today she found it irritating. "Shall we get started?"

"Certainly. Unless we're waiting for anyone else to join on your end."

"Who else might be joining us?"

"I would think that Walter might find time to be here. I am at the forefront of a major crisis. I thought he might have something to say on the matter."

"He has a great deal to say on the matter. Unfortunately, he is forced to say it to the media and government officials."

Gail felt the sting of his rebuke and it made her hackles rise. "Just what are you implying, Michael?"

"I'm not implying anything." A smile crept across his face. She could tell by the way it spread that he'd been hoping to say all this but wanted to bait her into starting the conversation. She'd fallen right into his poorly laid trap like a rookie. "With all due respect, Ms. Moore, you aren't at the forefront of this crisis. Mr. Compton is. Do you have any idea what he's been through trying to mitigate this PR disaster you've put us in?"

Heat rose in Gail's face and she knew Michael could see it. She hated herself and the betrayal of her body's reactions in moments like these. A man wouldn't blush like a little girl when he was angry, and she knew she lost credibility every time they saw her like this.

"I've put us in?"

"Are you not the Administrator of Moon Base? Are you not the individual Mr. Compton trusted with one of the most lucrative branches of his company? Aren't the secured personnel your responsibility?"

There it was, stated as clearly as anyone in the corporate world would ever state it. Andrus blamed her for this. That could only mean that, should things go poorly, they would blame her publicly. She did not trust that the reverse would be true. If things went well, Walter and the military would get the credit, not her. Her triumph, if there was one, would be part of the President's reelection bid and her name would never come up.

Gail gathered her thoughts before answering. A flashing in the corner of the screen reminded her that this conference was being recorded on the Andrus server. It may be her only chance to defend herself.

"Do you recall the last time we met like this?"

"I don't see how…"

"It was one month ago and I stated that there was a good deal of unrest among the prisoners."

"Secured personnel."

Gail choked on the term. It was created by Andrus to dress up the truth of their workforce. A corporate term that had neither meaning nor relevance when one saw the men in question in their apartments that looked like jail cells and their after-work strip searches.

"You'll recall that I have made a good number of requests for changes to our protocols. Not the least of which was one the ringleader Red complained about to Major Hawk this afternoon. Family visits and packages from home. You and I both know there has always been plenty of room on the cargo flights to accommodate more visitors. If we'd implemented any of the changes I recommended to make their lives better…"

Michael held up his hand and Gail actually saw him roll his eyes. Her cheeks burned brighter and her vision started to narrow, but she held her anger in check and let him speak.

"We can go back and forth all day about this, but the bottom line is that Andrus does not have inexhaustible resources. This incident has already ruined our quarterly numbers. We need to stop the bleeding."

The heat drained from her cheeks and the rest of her body. "What precisely do you mean?"

"It's time to cut our losses."

Gail tried to swallow, but her mouth felt full of sawdust. The matter-of-fact way he said that simple statement left her feeling terrified in a way she had not anticipated. This was why Walter wasn't here. He couldn't be recorded stating something so cold. Ordering deaths.

The truly terrifying fact was that Gail did not know what losses he meant to cut. He could have meant that she should order Major Hawk to make an all-out strike on the prisoners. Given the number of weapons involved, that would mean heavy losses on both sides. Given the military training of the Special Forces unit, the inevitable ending would be the death of all of the prisoners. She may not feel completely responsible for this crisis, but she did feel responsible for those men. She could not and would not allow their indiscriminate slaughter.

That was a terrible option, but it wasn't the worst option. He could mean that Andrus would cut off all aid and contact with the base. Cut all ties in a more concrete way. Abandon Moon Base and everyone there. The military would be recalled, of course, but there was not nearly enough room on their sky plane for all of Gail's people. Not without multiple trips, and Andrus's resources would be necessary for that authorization. She darted a look convulsively over her shoulder, checking the window for a retreating plane full of soldiers. The emptiness of the sky outside did little to reassure her.

Gail realized in that moment that she may not know exactly what Michael meant, but that she could not rule out any action. She would not have been surprised if he said they were cutting off all contact and letting everyone, civilian and prisoner alike, die up here. How did she end up working for a company like this? A company that she thought might be capable of murder in order to clean up their bottom line. Andrus may have had a reputation for ruthlessness, but it wasn't until this moment that she truly believed them to be heartless.

"Mr. Compton has been in touch with the President." Michael's voice came from a long way off. It was hollow as well as distant. "The military team has been authorized for full use of force."

"Could you explain that to me, please?"

"Major…" He quietly scanned a sheet of paper in front of him. "Major Hawk and his men have been authorized to eliminate all hostile targets immediately."

Gail didn't have time to correct him on Hawk's gender. He continued with details of the decision, who made it and when. She took notes, but none of it really mattered. The decision had come directly from the Pentagon.

Michael gave a clipped thank-you and an even more clipped wish for her good luck before ending the call. Gail sat staring at her reflection in the blank monitor for a long time. Thoughts tumbled through her brain and she did nothing to still them. She was unable to process the newly discovered shame in her employer. The fact that they had not gone with the most brutal option, but only the second most brutal option meant nothing to her. Knowing them capable of both changed the way she saw Andrus, but it also changed the way she saw herself.

She'd already known. That was the worst of it. If she allowed herself real honesty, she'd already known them capable of murder. Her ambition and her greed had brought her here and now she was reaping the rewards. Her mother had warned her of this. Had told her that some of the bulldozers sent in to clear out the protestors from Standing Rock sported Andrus logos. Gail had argued, reminding her mother that her company was the largest supplier of heavy machinery to the United States government. What the government did with their equipment after it was purchased was outside Andrus's control. She hadn't looked into it. She knew now why she hadn't. She didn't want to know.

Gail let her head fall into her hands and forced herself to think. She pulled up faces in her mind. She thought of Anderson, a thirtysomething prisoner who had a scar running down his left cheek. She'd thought it was from whatever crime he'd committed to earn himself a life sentence. After their third or fourth meeting during her inspections, she finally got him to speak and he told her that the scar had come from a car accident when he was nine years old. His father had lost control of the family's van and Anderson was orphaned that day. It wasn't a long road from foster homes to prison, even in Minneapolis, Minnesota.

He wasn't the only one with a story like that. Many of the men up here were monsters. Criminals who constituted a danger even if they dressed it up in smiles and charm the way Red had. Others were a victim of their circumstance. All of them were human beings who deserved to live. It was one of the reasons she'd wanted this job in the first place. A chance to prove that so many victims of the criminal justice system were merely people caught in a cycle they couldn't break on Earth. She could never give up on them. There had to be a way to save them.

A small sound made Gail lift her head. Beatrice stood in the open door, a coffee cup steaming in her white-knuckled grip. There was something in her eyes Gail did not often see, but worried about from all of her people. It was the same look she'd seen once in the eyes of a moose that had been hit on the side of the road. A tourist in a massive SUV had sped through the reservation without looking and smashed the moose's chest. The car sped off, but the moose lay moaning on the hot blacktop. Gail had approached slowly, all too aware of the erratic nature of wounded animals. She saw instantly in its eyes that it would be no threat to her. There was a wild panic in those black eyes that she saw again in Beatrice's blue. Her secretary knew she was going to die.

"Beatrice!" Gail hopped up, painting a welcoming smile on her face. "I'm sorry. I didn't see you come in."

Beatrice said nothing as Gail took the cup from her.

"I don't know how much of that you heard," Gail said, searching for but not receiving an answer. "But I don't want you to be worried."

"I'm…not worried," she squeaked.

"I know you are, though." Gail put a hand on her secretary's shoulder and felt her relax a fraction at the touch. "I am, too. I give you my word, I won't let anyone get hurt. You are perfectly safe."

Beatrice opened her mouth to speak, but closed it again and nodded, looking at her shoes. Gail wrapped her arm around her, holding her small body close to her side in a sort of half-hug. It was the most Gail could offer, but it seemed to settle Beatrice. When she looked back up, the fear had been replaced by resolve. Whether it was real or pretense in front of her boss was impossible to tell, but she would take strength from the resolve either way. For now, it was going to have to be enough.

"Do you know where I can find Major Hawk?" Gail asked gently.

If their previous interactions had been any indicator, Hawk would be hesitant to make a violent move. If Gail could get to her in time, there may be some way to stop this whole thing. Perhaps she could convince the major to wait.

"She requested a conference room," Beatrice answered, her voice noticeably stronger than before. "She wanted to call her superior."

Gail knew Beatrice saw her face fall. It was clear in her new expression. Disappointment shone there with the same inevitability Gail felt. She hurried out of the room without as much as a thank you for the coffee.

CHAPTER THIRTEEN

"What do you think, crazy or evil?"

Hawk massaged the bridge of her nose. She tried to remember the last time she'd slept and decided she'd been awake for at least thirty hours. Her soldiers were either all sacked out or on patrol. Even her officers were out for their mandated rest. Instead of catching up on sleep herself, she was sitting alone in a conference room staring at a computer screen.

General Carter Harris, her CO and mentor, was usually a comfort to her. Not so tonight. The angle of his jaw and eyebrows communicated disappointment and annoyance. She had no idea whether they were caused by her actions or something completely unrelated. He rarely shared the cause of his emotions, even to her.

"Neither, sir. Well, maybe evil, but certainly not crazy. Manipulative. Narcissistic. A man with a dangerously elevated self-worth and a host of thugs and killers that he has wrapped around his little finger."

"You're saying he can't be reasoned with?"

"I'm saying he has nothing to lose and he's convinced those around him think the same. If there was someone close to him that might make a bid for power, I'd have something to work with, but I don't know enough about these people."

"The Administrator can't give you access to their prison files?"

Hawk rubbed her neck and looked back at Harris. His eyes seemed softer now. Maybe they always had been and she'd only seen her own frustration there. "She doesn't have full access to them. The whole idea of bringing these men up here was that they got a clean slate. No one knows what they did, no one can judge them on their past, only their work."

"You think she's telling you the truth?"

Hawk narrowed her eyes. "He wanted me to hand her over as a goddamn sex slave to a bunch of murderers and rapists. Believe me, sir, she is fully cooperative."

He held up his hands in surrender. "Whoa, Charlie, bring it down a notch. I'm sure she's being as cooperative as she can, but keep in mind that you are talking to the mouthpiece for the richest and most powerful corporation on the planet and beyond. She didn't get there by being a Girl Scout."

As a throb cut through her head again, Hawk bit back her anger. "She's telling the truth."

He squinted at her, peeling her apart and reading her like a book. It was the same thing he did in the hills of Kandahar when she was one of only a handful of women in combat. Same thing he did when she became the first woman to qualify for Special Forces assignment. Same thing he did when he handed off his elite Company to her and went to USSOCOM.

"We'll shelve that for now. Let's operate as if his motives are unresolved. What is your assessment of the men around him?"

"A good number could be classified as nonviolent, but they're all on death row, so they did something big to get themselves here. There are definitely some that will be trouble, but enough level heads to keep most civilians out of danger. I could see it in their eyes. Most of them don't want a fight, but they won't make too much trouble with their own. Bottom line is they want this place, they think they deserve it and they have enough weapons to make it a messy takedown. The good news is we are effectively in a stalemate. They can't do anything more from where they are, and, unless we force it, there is no reason to believe there will be armed conflict."

"What about his threat? About when you cross the horizon?"

"The dark horizon. The spot in the Moon's rotation where we start a period of fourteen days of darkness. No sunlight for two weeks. Only battery power to sustain life." She picked up her cold coffee and drank deeply from it, despite the bitter, burnt thickness at the bottom of the cup. "If they make a move, they'll wait until then. We'll be more vulnerable and the complex will be significantly darker. We'll have communication with Earth satellites for about three hours after. But that's all. Then we're alone."

"Right, well…" He shuffled some papers on his desk, his eyes fixed on them instead of the screen. "The official decision down here is that you should delay as long as possible, but, if there is no resolution by the time you reach dark horizon, you are to attack with full use of force."

"What?" Hawk set her cup down more abruptly than she had intended, the ceramic clunking loudly on the wooden table. "Carter, that's crazy. They're a bunch of idiots with a cult leader! That should be the last option. Give me more time to resolve this."

"There is no more time. Red planned his attack well."

"That's not enough to work with. You can't send me up here with a mission and then change the parameters so quickly."

"I didn't change them. The enemy did."

"We're letting the enemy dictate our strategy now?"

He looked back up into the camera, and there was exhaustion in his eyes. As he spoke, the door behind Hawk opened. "Those are your orders, Major, and they come from a hell of a lot higher than me. Someone who I cannot argue with. Short guy, fancy suits, lives north of Virginia, south of Maryland. Goes by the name Commander in Chief."

"This is premature, General."

He leaned forward, his finger hovering over the keyboard of his computer. "Then you better figure out another escape route soon, Charlie."

His finger came down with a click and the screen went blank. She stared at her desktop, fighting both her annoyance and the headache that had now firmly planted itself behind her eyeballs.

"I take it you've been informed of the decision?"

Hawk swiveled her chair around to look at Gail. The woman looked just as fresh and composed as she had the moment they met face to face twelve hours ago. Not a hair was out of place, not a wrinkle in her suit. Her face was still stubbornly neutral, her hands clasped behind her back and her shoulders straight. Her seemingly unconcerned demeanor caused another jolt of pain through Hawk's head. She just wanted to sleep.

"I have. I take it your people are behind this?"

"It seems so, yes." She moved to a chair across from Hawk and smoothed the back of her skirt as she sat down. "Our Board of Directors has determined that the public relations nightmare of a prolonged firefight would reflect more negatively on our image than a swift reprisal. Especially if there are unintended casualties."

"Unintended casualties?" Hawk raised an eyebrow and her fist clenched hard around her coffee mug. "I take it you are referring to your people and mine? Mostly mine since we'll be the ones carrying out this...what was the term you used earlier? 'Clean sweep?'"

"Our security forces will, of course, offer their full support. Though, as you pointed out earlier, this is a military operation now."

A wave of disappointment flooded through Hawk, and her exhaustion and frustration allowed it to take a firm hold. "Is that the way the land lies then? You aren't willing to let Drumm do the dirty work—that would put blood on your hands. So, what, you encourage the powers that be to put this on me? Make my men do it? Make me give the order?"

Gail sat as still as a figure carved into a mountain. "You flatter me to think I have that much influence over the will of my superiors." Finally her eyes flicked away, settling on a painting of a sailboat perched atop a thickly painted wave. "In fact, Major, I have found out today just how much weight my voice loses as it travels back to Earth."

Her headache had become white noise, still present but easier to ignore. "You don't suppose Drumm…"

"No, Derek has no clout with the company. I would be surprised if they even knew his name in New York." She tapped her fingers on the tabletop, her nails clicking rhythmically. Resignation flooded out of her pores. "No, I suspect that these events were set into motion before your team even left the planet. Our CEO is a master… Still, the idea that they would take this step when there hasn't been a single death, is unexpected."

It took time for Hawk's mind to grind back into gear. "You expected this."

It wasn't a question, and Gail looked quizzically at her. "You're military. Special Forces. Surely you expected they were sending you up here for a battle?"

"No, actually, I didn't." Further explanation was required, and she forced herself to be as clear as she could. "Since the end of open conflict in Asia, Charlie Company has been focused on more…unconventional warfare. Counterterrorism, hostage rescue. Those are the missions we typically deploy for, not open conflict. We just spent a month squatting in a jungle in Brazil to watch over an NGO's work with at-risk indigenous people. We aren't the group you send in if you want a strike force."

Gail looked at her stonily, but Hawk almost imagined the woman looked impressed. "Then it seems we are both bound to be disappointed by this mission."

She stood and Hawk followed. "That's it? You're giving up that easily?"

"What can we do? We both have orders."

Despite the reduced gravity on the Moon, Hawk felt the weight of her long day and leaned against the table. "Our superiors are a long way from here."

She had almost hoped for a smile, but Gail did not oblige. "Is that how you've attained your current rank? By disobeying orders?"

"Not disobeying. Massaging. And yes, it is. I know most people think we're all just mindless automatons, but the Army values a nimble mind as much as a Fortune 500 company does."

"As of last year Andrus Industries owns *Fortune Magazine*." Her eyes went back to the sailboat. "Besides, a nimble mind is not as highly favored there as you might think."

"It is with me. When do we cross dark horizon?"

Gail looked at her watch. "Twenty-seven minutes ago."

"Then we have fourteen days until they find out what we've done."

Gail crossed her arms. "Is that a good thing or a bad thing?"

"Depends on how much power Red really has."

The sentence had not fully left her lips when the room around them blinked into darkness.

CHAPTER FOURTEEN

A darkness so absolute that it had substance stole over Gail. The weight of it pressed against her eyes even as she opened them as wide as she could. The absolute cold of deep space wrapped its arms around her and all the oxygen left the air. She was suffocating and freezing to death and she was utterly blind. Her arm shot out in panic, trying to find something, anything to hold on to and keep her tethered to the spark of life still inside her. Her fingertips hit something soft and warm and she clawed at it with a vice-like grip. Softness balled in her fist and warm muscle bunched. Hawk let out a grunt of pain, but Gail just squeezed tighter, raking her fingernails through the woman's flesh.

Just as the world started to fade around the edges and her lungs screamed with the inability to expand, half the lights flicked back on. A humming filled her ears as the heating system ground back into life. The air around her was suddenly breathable again and she gulped in huge, wonderful mouthfuls. She looked into Hawk's face and the concern there showed her just how wild she must appear.

"Ms. Moore?"

Heat bloomed across her neck and she shifted her gaze to her hand. It was gripping tight at Hawk's abdomen. Her uniform jacket and T-shirt had come loose from the waistband of her pants and Gail could see pink scratches across the firm plane of her stomach where it was exposed.

Hawk's hand came to rest on her shoulder. "Gail? Are you okay?"

Her world was resetting as slowly as the heating system, but at least it was happening now. She relaxed her hand and stepped back. She tried to speak but her throat was still frozen. She cleared her throat and tried again. "I… Sorry. I was…caught by surprise."

Another long moment under that searching stare and Gail found she had to move. She walked around the table to the panel on the wall, wrenching the phone from its cradle, and with shaky hands, punched a series of numbers. The line was dead.

"They cut the power. How did they manage that so quickly?"

"I don't know, but it shouldn't have happened." Gail made for the door, her poise restored by movement. "Follow me."

To her credit, Hawk didn't argue. She followed swiftly, a few steps behind Gail as they wound their way through corridors. Gail used her thorough knowledge of the facility to calculate the route as she moved, avoiding elevators and ID card-locked doors. She didn't know whether the security system would lock them open or closed on this side of the compound and she didn't want to waste time finding out.

When she opened a service corridor access and found a yawning blackness, she froze. Hawk stepped forward without missing a beat, yanking a powerful flashlight from her belt.

"Okay?"

Gail nodded and moved on, cursing herself silently for her poor reaction. They didn't have time for her weakness and she did her best to force it down. Later, when this was all over and her people were safe, she would open up that jar of fear and let it wash over her. But not now. She could not afford to show weakness in front of Hawk. This woman knew true bravery and so she must know true cowardice. What she couldn't know yet was the fear of living in a place where one crack in the glass, one lax inspection, meant suffocation for dozens of people. She'd know it soon enough, though. Now that the power was out, the line between life and death for all of them was the gossamer strand of a spider's web.

They quickly chewed up the distance to the first floor, darting down hallways and staircases with a speed borne of anxiety. When they encountered another pitch-black service corridor on the second floor, Gail didn't flinch. The minor victory over her anxiety was only slightly marred by the hand Hawk put on her shoulder blade as she flipped on the flashlight. Hawk no doubt meant it to be supportive, but she found it closer to pitying.

Gail couldn't deny the comfort of her hand though. There was a subtle intimacy to it that excited her. She couldn't recall the last time anyone touched her more than a handshake. She focused on the feeling as they finally neared the Forward Staging Area close to the cafeteria.

They heard gunshots before they reached the end of the corridor, and Hawk broke into a run, pulling her sidearm from her hip as she stopped at the corner. She waited, listening, and then peeked her head out just enough to scan for a split second before pulling back to safety. Gail came to a stop, panting, beside her.

"Stay here until I send for you."

"What's…"

"Stay here until I send for you."

With that Hawk ducked around the corner and hurried off at a half-crouch. Gail found herself reluctant to leave the soldier's side, but another burst of gunfire kept her back. There was muffled shouting and popping that sounded to her like distant firecrackers. She could feel her heart rate pick up, and the thought of that impenetrable blackness of the conference room engulfed her. She felt the cold again, and her neck started to tingle as the hairs stood on end. She took a step back at the next clatter of weapons. The shouting grew louder and so did the pound of her pulse in her ears.

Gail picked out what she thought was Hawk's voice among the shouting and felt marginally better. Then she realized the hall had become silent. The shouting had stopped, the gunfire had stopped. She waited, counting to ten once and then again to calm herself. On the third repetition she heard running from around the corner. She took another step back, looking around and realizing she had nothing with which to defend herself.

A young soldier with wide, cold eyes under the brim of her helmet turned the corner, an assault rifle held loosely across her armored chest. After a moment, Gail recognized her face from their brief encounter at the communication table yesterday.

"We need a medic."

The battle scene was a mess of blood and concrete dust. The two mingled into black mud that Gail tried to avoid as she picked her way down the hall. There was an array of pock marks in the walls. She watched a trickle of gray-white dust fall from the holes. She looked at them with a sense of detached fascination, her mind painting the picture of one of those swarm of bullets tearing through the concrete and out through the three layers of glass. She imagined oxygen leaking out through that hole and then the pressure bursting the trickle into a flood, tearing through glass and concrete and flesh and emptying them all into the fatal lunar desert.

She turned away before it could crack her self-control. She had already lost her grip once today, and it would not happen again. Her gaze settled on the three bundles, lined up and covered in white sheets against the far wall. She hadn't seen their faces before the soldiers covered them and she was relieved. The uncharitable corner of her mind wondered what they had done to lose their freedom. What had led to them signing a contract to exchange a prison on Earth for a prison on the Moon? And the worst thought, the one that would have made her hate herself if she had the luxury of such self-indulgence, was the world better off without them?

Near the bodies was a cluster of soldiers, Major Hawk somewhere among them. The base's doctor, summoned when the skirmish ended, worked industriously over the moaning mass at the middle of the group. The soldiers huddled close were making themselves as helpful as they could in tending the fallen man. Gail assumed it was a soldier, one of their own that they were fighting hard to save. Whoever it was and whatever they were doing, she felt out of place in this group, and she was exhausted. She wondered whether it was appropriate for her to slip away to her apartment and fall into bed. The only thing holding her in place was needing to know how the prisoners had managed to get out here and cut the main power lines.

CHAPTER FIFTEEN

Hawk knelt among her soldiers, some standing and some lying in a pool of blood and tried to piece together exactly what had happened in the chaos of the last hour. The details were only now coming together. She stayed very still and very quiet, allowing her mind to sort through it all.

One thing was clear at least. Red had an inside man. Someone on the civilian side who helped those three dead prisoners escape their barricaded corridor, avoid all her patrols and make it to this hallway. This was the only spot where they could have cut the power to the civilian side while leaving their own half of the dome intact, and that was why this corridor had earned so much attention from Hawk and her team. Yet somehow these three men made it here.

She squatted next to the row of neatly lined white sheets and tried to work it all out, staring into the middle distance, spinning scenarios and discarding them one by one. Occasionally her eyes fell on the shrouds and her fury simmered beneath her placid face. She hated casualties, her own or the enemy's, it didn't matter. She didn't want people dying on her watch. The only way to prevent more deaths was to figure out how these came to be. She started at the beginning again, willing herself to tease a new thread lose.

As she and Gail had maneuvered through the dome from the conference room upstairs to the Forward Staging Area, Hawk had called Forest on their personal comms. The decision to bring their own communications system with its own power supply suddenly seemed prescient. The fact that Forest had been the one to insist on that precaution did not save him from Hawk's loud, angry rebuke. She'd left him in charge while she contacted General Harris and so the incursion happened on his watch.

He'd insisted that no one had come through the barricade and, what was more, the airtight door closest to the barricade on the civilian side had just slid shut, providing an impenetrable barrier for civilian and prisoner alike. The breach hadn't come through there. They'd found another way in.

When Forest's team tried to reopen the door, the controls were unresponsive. Not even the override commands Derek Drumm had provided had worked. They had ceased trying when the firefight started, but there wasn't much they could do. They were locked out.

This realization brought another crashing down on Hawk. One far more troubling than a stubborn security system. They were now completely cut off from the prisoner side. They'd crossed the dark horizon and communications with Earth were now impossible. The prisoners had full power whereas the civilian side was now limited to the backup batteries. All Red had to do was wait them out. The clock was ticking.

In seven days, she and all her people would be dead.

Hawk pushed that thought aside. She couldn't become bogged down in fear, not while she still couldn't see the full picture. The moment she arrived, she'd run smack into the fight between her sentry platoon and the three prisoners. It had been far more of a fight than it should have been. Three prisoners against fifteen trained soldiers, but there were half a dozen members of Charlie Company writhing on the ground, waiting for the company medic or the base doctor to get to them. It was hard to believe so many of them had been injured by so few, but the scene was confusion from beginning to end.

It had not been a coordinated attack. Hawk could tell that even before she pulled her sidearm and told Gail to stay out of it. The shouting as she rounded the corner seemed as much shock as anything else, and they were mostly coming from her own men. A surprise ambush. There was no cover in the hallway, and the whole thing descended into a shooting gallery immediately.

Hawk pieced together a timeline from the scattered reports, gathering that the prisoners had come out of the hallway's single door at exactly the wrong moment. The door led to the power junction box, and so was an obvious target. Hawk had set a series of sentry parties to patrol the area at regular intervals. This group had taken a wrong turn on their sweep and had to double back on their assigned route, putting them here much later than they should have been.

The soldiers were feet away from the door when it opened and the startled prisoners poured out, bumping headlong into them. The prisoners recovered from their shock an instant faster and now Private Thompson had a tourniquet around his thigh and a deep gash across his forehead. He was alive, a miracle attributed to the prisoners' lack of training. From the ground Thompson killed the first man as the hall around him exploded in noise and blood. Hawk watched him squirm as the base doctor pressed a square of gauze against the gaping head wound.

Shifting her attention back to the line of bodies, Hawk tried to envisage how they managed this. It was a terrible plan if you were one of the unlucky three who had to carry it out. There had never been much of a chance they'd live to see their fellow rebels again, and the botched patrol route only shortened the odds. Of course for Red, it was a complete victory. He got the upper hand logistically, having achieved his aim of turning off the power to the civilian side, and had the bonus of cementing Hawk as the enemy. Hawk's soldiers would be gripping their weapons tighter every moment one of their own was in the infirmary. There was bloodshed and anger on both sides. Exactly what Hawk had been trying to avoid and there was no turning back.

No turning back. The phrase tumbled around in her mind as she stood and watched the base doctor Samuel Nguyen, a small Asian man in black scrubs, move from Thompson to the next wounded soldier.

It had been a suicide mission for Red to send these men blindly into enemy territory. He could certainly devise the basic attack on his own but carrying it out would be impossible without someone to let the team through locked ventilation shafts or maintenance tunnels. Someone who knew how to avoid the patrols set at key areas, including the corridor with the power controls. Someone who could be overlooked. Hawk was back to the insider.

Hawk's first thought was the menacing reference Red made to women among the corporate staff who would come to him willingly. That felt wrong though. Incomplete. Sex wasn't a strong enough motive to risk one's life, no matter how good the sex. It had to be someone with a stronger motive. She'd tried to question the one prisoner still alive but all he could give was a bloody smile and slip away into death.

A clang of metal dropping onto concrete cut through the quiet of the hall. Hawk's sidearm was in her hand before she had time for a conscious thought. She held it lightly in her grasp, muzzle pointed at the floor in front of the single closed door. The sound had come from inside. She hadn't checked it when the fighting stopped and now she was cursing herself for the oversight.

With a pair of quick, silent hand motions she instructed two of her soldiers to take the doctor out of danger. She shot a quick look over her shoulder to where she'd last seen Gail. The Administrator was still leaning against the wall at the end of the hallway, looking exhausted and scared. She jerked her head at another soldier and she went to protect Gail from whatever threat was in this closet. Without prompting, a pair of soldiers flanked the door, weapons ready.

Hawk reached for the door handle with her left hand, gripping her weapon firmly in her right. She yanked it open with a swift motion and transferred the hand back to her sidearm, ready for attack. None came.

Sitting propped against the wall, looking pale and weak, was someone Hawk recognized. It took her a moment to shuffle through the memories and locate his name. Stone. The reporter from the plane. He had both hands pressed to separate spots low on his abdomen. Blood seeped between his fingers in rivulets like a trickle from a melting iceberg.

Her soldiers sprang into action, checking him and the room for weapons. Hawk knew they wouldn't find one. She stowed her sidearm slowly, watching Stone's face fade to a lighter pale. He slid a little further down the wall as her soldiers checked his pockets and under his shirt.

"Clear," one of them announced and they both stepped back.

The base doctor rushed over, pushing her soldier out of the way. He pulled a pair of blue nitrile gloves over his small hands as Hawk stepped forward.

"Help me get him out of here."

Hawk had expected the doctor's voice to be small and high to match his stature, but it wasn't. He had the authoritative ring of a man used to being in charge.

Hawk snatched one of Stone's ankles and yanked. He slid easily into the corridor, his shoulder and head making a wet thunk against the concrete as they lost the support of the wall. She tried not to take too much satisfaction in that sound or in the disapproving look from the doctor. Not until the doctor shouted for his nurse did Hawk realize there was another civilian in the crowd. She was quick to move to his side, a nylon bag of medical supplies in her gloved hand.

Stone was unconscious now, his face set in a grimace and the color continuing to pull back from it. The final piece fit into place. The inside man. The only question was: why?

"Is he going to live?"

The doctor didn't look up. "Too soon to tell."

Movement caught Hawk's eye. Her company medic moved to the soldier the base doctor had abandoned mid-treatment. The patient groaned, blood running down the left side of his face. Sergeant Mateo Grace from Hoboken, care of Puerto Rico. His mother sent homemade panetela cake to Hawk last Christmas. Several other men were nursing small injuries, mostly from flying debris. She hadn't seen this many members of Charlie Company wounded in a long time. The sight added a log to her fire of anger.

She should have anticipated this. Should have known Red wouldn't wait behind a stack of furniture and let the Army overtake his domain. She had spent less than an hour in his company and she already knew he was a man of action who would never let her make the first move. She should have been better prepared. She should have secured the area. There were a hundred thousand things she could have done to save lives, but she had her mind set on a peaceful resolution. She had been wrong and they were paying for it now.

Looking up the hallway, she saw again the set, wan face of Gail Moore. It was easy, looking at her now, to imagine the panic of the other civilians. They had crossed the dark horizon, the power was cut and the clock was ticking on the backup batteries.

Hawk clenched her jaw and turned back to Dr. Nguyen, struggling to save the reporter. "Make sure he lives."

CHAPTER SIXTEEN

A few hours' sleep did nothing to improve Hawk's mood. The number of deployments she had experienced in her long career made a cot in a tent just as comfortable as a bed at home, but her mind was too active to allow exhaustion to lull her to sleep. She stared into the dark, her thoughts buzzing almost audibly, and, when sleep did finally take her, it was brief and unfulfilling. Her eyes snapped open at the appointed time, and she readied herself with efficiency rather than interest.

She arrived at the base's medical clinic to find Administrator Moore waiting for her. The woman looked a little rested, but the barely concealed dark circles under slightly glassy eyes suggested that her sleep may have been aided by pharmaceuticals. Still, her suit was neatly pressed and she stood erect. Hawk looked for the panic that had overcome her when the power went out, but if it was present, it was carefully in check. The corporate mask was firmly in place again as she reached out to shake Hawk's hand by way of a morning greeting.

Dr. Nguyen could have passed for a middle schooler. His khakis were wrinkled and his tie had such a large knot that it looked like a clip on. His raven black hair might have been cut sitting on a stool in his mother's kitchen. He explained at great length that he was not a surgeon, but an emergency medicine doctor. He had only signed up for this because Andrus had promised to pay off his entire student loan in return for just one year at Moon Base. He was adamant that he had clearly paid his dues and he expected to be relieved of his position and be on the next flight home. Hawk cut him off, requesting a description of Stone's injuries. The bullets had nicked the left kidney. Nguyen had to remove it. His nurse was shell-shocked after the encounter.

Hawk let Gail placate the doctor. She was more concerned with Stone. To her surprise, the patient appeared to be recovering well. He likely would not have the energy for a long conversation, so Gail and she were allowed ten minutes with him. They could ask the nurse any questions on their way out since Dr. Ngyuen was going back to his room and would be unavailable for a few hours.

Stone certainly did not look well. His ruddy face was the pale yellow of fresh butter, and he looked sunken. Diminished somehow. He lay absolutely still, his chest rising only a few shuddering inches before dropping again. Hawk had to shout his name several times and give his shoulder a none-too-gentle shake before he peeled his eyes open with obvious difficulty. He blinked and his eyes met hers, but there was no sense in them. The whites showed and they closed again. Again Hawk shook him awake, and this time it stuck a bit longer.

"Do you remember what happened in the corridor? There were prisoners there, and my men. Do you remember firing a gun at the soldiers?"

He blinked and, with each pass, his eyelids seemed to clear away some of the confusion. He nodded and swallowed hard, trying to speak.

"What was that, Stone? Say it again, I couldn't hear you."

Hawk leaned over, but the man had found his voice and she could hear him at last. "Loves me..."

"What are you talking about, Stone? What happened? Why can't we turn the power back on? We tried the consoles you used, but they're locked out. The other stations aren't responding either. What did you do?"

His smile was weak, but smug. "Caesar... Protocol."

Hawk looked over Stone's shoulder at the nurse in the corner. "What drugs do you have him on? He's not making any sense."

Gail cleared her throat. "He is, actually. Caesar Protocol is a safeguard in the computer system. It allows for the entire network to be completely locked down and access granted to a single terminal."

Stone's eyes were losing focus again. "Checkmate."

"How do we get the systems back online?"

"We don't." Gail looked at the ground, her cheeks hollowing and her jaw clenching. "The Protocol is meant to be a last resort failsafe. In the event of a catastrophic environmental failure or an armed assault. It is irreversible without access to the Caesar Terminal."

"The power cut was...manual...but there are...bypass...you lose...should have...taken his terms..."

"We'll discuss that more later. Right now there are other pressing matters." She turned back to Stone and shook him so hard he hissed in pain. "What are the prisoners planning?"

"Not planning. Just...going to wait."

"Wait for what?"

He swallowed hard again and grimaced. "For you to...leave."

Hawk had been so focused on the man in the bed that the sound of Gail's voice startled her. "We can't leave, Mr. Stone. Cutting the power means the airlock for the plane can't open. The air exchange inside won't work, so the hangar doors automatically lock down. He knows that. He splits his time between the livestock pod and The Docks. He would know we can't get out. All we can do is die."

Stone furrowed his brow again. "No one dies...that was... plan. You're...wrong."

Hawk glared at him, and Stone grimaced in pain. "And you find him trustworthy?"

"Loves me..."

"You said that before. Who loves you? Red? He left you here to die with the rest of us."

"No." It was a whisper, but there was weight to the word. "Mistake...you...too early... He loves...me."

Gail spoke before Hawk could, and there was something like tenderness in her voice. "Who is he, Mr. Stone? How did you fall in love with him?"

"Not...like that..." Fat tears sprung to the corner of his eyes and fell slowly as he spoke, "I found him...my mother... when she died, she told me." He swallowed again, and seemed to gain some strength by telling the story. "Didn't know she was pregnant. She wrote, but he went to prison. She got married. Her husband...hurt us both. I ran away... She found me a few years ago. Told me about Red... I wrote him...already signed the contract...he was...proud of me."

Hawk didn't need the subtle movement from the nurse to know it was time to go. Stone was slipping out of consciousness. His cracked lips moved, but no sound came from them. She moved to the door without a backward glance, and the soft click of the administrator's heels followed her from the room.

"What do you think?" Hawk asked when they were alone.

"We're going to die."

Hawk leaned against the wall outside the Clinic, arms crossed over her chest, and Gail stood at the railing looking out into the vast dark. The Clinic entrance was along an outer wall, and so for the first time since standing on the viewing deck at the top of dome, Hawk was able to see outside the building. Gail stared at the sight, transfixed by the deep dark and the soft glow from the farming pod in the distance.

"That's not going to happen."

"I wish I had your confidence."

Hawk looked at the farming pod. It still had full power. Stone's sabotage had only affected the main building.

"Can we get over there?"

"No, each structure was intended to be self-contained in the event of loss of environment. There is only one access point." She spread her arms along the railing and slumped visibly. "It's on the prisoner's side. So is access to the livestock pod."

"What about the mining pod?"

"We have access from here, but an airlock door came down just like the corridor to the prisoners. Those doors are strong enough to hold out the vacuum of space. I doubt we can breach them. We're sealed in tight."

"Maintenance tunnels?"

"Sealed."

"What about exterior access?"

"There are airlocks at intervals along the passageway. One could be opened and we could get in through there. The problem is we would have about a mile hike along the surface to get there."

"I think your people can handle a mile hike if it means saving their lives."

Gail sighed and turned, leaning heavily on the railing, "Of course, but there is no oxygen out there. We would have to wear the space suits our miners use. There are a dozen of them in The Docks, and that's it. I have twenty-seven people here counting myself. You?"

"One hundred six."

Gail shook her head. "It just wouldn't work. The suits are too fragile to be packed up and carried back and forth. Ten people getting in and out of them. Even a small tear would be enough to kill the person wearing it."

"Okay, no evacuation that way. You said the hangar doors are shut down, so no flying out of here."

"No, Major. I'm afraid we're stuck here." She turned back to the window. "Like I said, we're going to die."

Hawk stood upright and walked over to the railing, anger flaring. "We don't need that sort of attitude, Administrator

Moore. You need to focus on a solution. Your people need you. I need you. Don't let this asshole get the better of you."

When she looked at Hawk Gail's eyes were still hard as a block of amber, but they were dry.

CHAPTER SEVENTEEN

Gail's life was becoming repetitive. At least it felt that way, with her spending yet another morning walking through the abandoned halls of the corporate housing block. Yesterday morning she'd felt an optimistic sort of confidence, now she was merely projecting confidence she did not feel. After the power had been cut, she addressed her staff, informing them in a limited way about the current situation. She knew a version of the truth might quell rumors for a while, so she put as rosy a spin on it as she could. Then they'd gone back to their rooms alone to sleep and worry. It wasn't yet clear how effective her speech had been.

Major Hawk had imposed a curfew, sending all the civilians back to their rooms as soon as the meeting had ended. Gail led them all up here, keeping an inconspicuous eye on their body language. Knowing each of these men and women as she did, she was shocked at how few showed signs of alarm or outright panic. It seemed prudent to keep a close watch, just in case their reactions were delayed. So far, the rooms had all been quiet.

The calm was a blessing, and not just because it meant her people were adjusting well. She needed the calm to quiet her own fears. Her own pessimism. The Caesar Protocol had been activated. That little bit of news had been the biggest shock. Even more than the power being cut. It was a far bigger hurdle than Major Hawk realized.

Piecing together the string of events, Gail figured out what had happened step-by-step. Because it was a last resort, and irreversible, Andrus had given only a handful of computer terminals authority to initiate the Caesar Protocol. Three of them were in the office suite where Gail and Hawk had been speaking before the power was cut. Three more were in the living quarters heavily guarded by both Drumm's men and Hawk's. The others were scattered throughout the main floor so these were the most likely candidates. There were none on the prisoner side. A similarly small number of terminals could be assigned the duties of Caesar Terminal. There were computers with the authority on the prison side in case an evacuation to that side were necessary.

Caesar had to have been initiated from this side and it followed that it had to happen before the power was cut, disabling the computers. For his plan to succeed, Red had to send a team across to the civilian side with specific instructions to complete complicated procedures. How could he have known which terminals could access Caesar? How had he even known how to execute them? Stone could have used his journalist credentials to access a floorplan, but the Caesar Protocol was a closely guarded secret. He couldn't have known.

The plan required pinpoint timing and a great deal of insider knowledge. The timing aspect bothered her because it showed input from a keen intellect. She knew Red was smart, but there was a difference between smart and methodical. This plan was certainly the latter. It required patience and deliberation, disproving his assertion that the rebellion had been a spontaneous act brought on by prisoner discontent. Red had planned this, seeking out classified information and strategy long before his men refused their work details.

The knowledge aspect was far more troubling. Most of Gail's staff were unaware of the Caesar Protocol. It was a failsafe created for the direst emergencies. Only a handful of the executive staff were aware of it and only three individuals had the codes required to initiate it. Hers were etched into an aluminum plate shaped like a military dog tag that hung around her neck at all times.

Similar tags were worn by Stephanie Gilliard, Director of Engineering and de facto second in command, and Randy Phelps, Director of Information and Technology. Neither was beyond reproach. Gilliard was meek and Phelps tended toward forgetfulness. Still, neither was likely to form a friendship with Red. Gilliard had never ventured into the prisoner wing and had confided to Gail that she was afraid of the prisoners. Phelps was devoted to his wife, who also lived on Moon Base, and would never do anything to put her in danger. Not purposefully.

Just last month there was a software update to the system and a new set of tags was sent from Earth. As soon as her secretary handed her the package, Gail had distributed the other two their new tags and confiscated the old. She destroyed them later that day in the machine room. Last night she'd checked with Gilliard and Phelps and they both had their tags secured. Both had also looked her in the eye and demanded she not enact Caesar. They were concerned about the implications if the prisoners died as a consequence. There was nothing but truth in their eyes. They hadn't betrayed her to Red.

The question became: who did? How much did they know about the true nature of Caesar? Did they realize they'd handed a murderer a weapon that could kill everyone here, including themselves? Would Red explore the commands enough to realize the extent of his power? Caesar allowed him to override redundant security, remotely blow exterior doors or even shut down oxygen scrubbing. Any number of gruesome deaths were a keystroke away for all of them now.

Passing an apartment door, Gail heard the muffled sound of sobbing. It was faint, so she stopped to be sure she hadn't imagined it. She hadn't. It came again, the quiet wail of fear and loneliness. She knew the sound well. When she'd last heard a sound like that, it came from her grandmother's room. That wail had mixed with the rhythmic pound of drums and the soft insistence of family members that her grandmother come out and stand tall at her husband's funeral. Gail had been too small to understand the sound then. To her, it sounded like the usual, ululating voices of song that accompanied the drums.

This was Beatrice's room. Her secretary was crying in fear. Gail raised her hand to knock but thought better of it. She was still swimming in her own doubt. She was in no position to comfort someone else. She lowered her hands, smoothing her blazer instead. Gail would check on her later.

Gail moved on, allowing her mind to wander back to Red, who was now Caesar. She peered over the railing as she walked, trying to penetrate the dark to see across the dome. The security gates and impenetrable walls between civilian and prisoner housing had always been in place, they were just more decorative here than anywhere else. She could see into the prisoners' domain, full of light and warmth, but it was as inaccessible as Earth. No doubt Red enjoyed looking across this expanse and glorying in their eventual demise. She wondered if he would restore power and light after all the civilians were dead. Would they come over here and remove the bodies and take the more comfortable quarters for themselves?

Mentally cursing herself, Gail pushed the thought aside. This walk had been to clear her head and restore her hope, not to wallow in dark thoughts. A voice called out behind her.

"Gail?" Randy Phelps stepped out of his apartment, pulling the door quietly shut behind him. His wife was an associate in the Accounting Department. She must have been asleep inside, based on the care Randy took to be quiet as he approached Gail.

She looked him over closely, trying to confirm, now that they were face-to-face, her instincts about his loyalty. He was wearing an old pair of jeans and a ratty white T-shirt. Randy was usually as buttoned up as they came. He didn't wear suits, but his khakis were always crisply ironed and his shirts always smelled heavily of starch. Seeing him so casually dressed was jarring, but it also convinced her of his innocence. A traitor would not be able to look her in the eye, but he was as calm and warm as ever.

"Can't sleep, Randy?"

He kept his voice low, as she had done, even though he was now standing next to her across the hall from his sleeping wife. "Too cold in there. Annie always likes it a little cold, so when the environmental controls took us down a few degrees from our already low preset, it was rough."

It was the most natural thing in the world, a couple fighting over the thermostat, but there was a sinister edge to the conversation up here. They were all going to get a lot colder before this was all over.

"Doesn't bother her though, huh?"

Randy laughed, then caught himself and lowered his volume. "She'd sleep in a refrigerator if she could."

Gail smiled, thinking of her own ex and how they'd fought this out. Gail grew up in the desert without the luxury of air-conditioning. Her first apartment had a window unit, and she would turn it up to full blast in the summer and sit naked in front of it, delighting in the chill bumps on her skin.

"I'm afraid I'll have to side with Annie on this one," she said, earning another soft laugh from this bear of a man.

"You women always stick together." After a heartbeat of hesitation he asked, "Speaking of, what do you think of Major Hawk?"

Gail swallowed down the true answer—that she was gorgeous and infuriating and Gail hated to think that she was going to die up here on the Moon. It was such a waste of a fine woman. Instead, she replied, "She's very good at what she does. We have nothing to worry about, Randy. Major Hawk will save us."

"I'm not worried," he said with such casualness it was almost flippant. Watching him, Gail realized he really wasn't worried.

He turned his eyes on her and she saw confidence. Determination. Good to see. If Randy wasn't scared, then quite probably, Annie wasn't scared. If Annie wasn't scared then it was a good bet most of the others weren't scared either. It warmed Gail's heart to know that her people were okay.

"I better get back in there or Annie'll worry. Good night, Gail."

"Good night, Randy," she said to his back.

She saw a soldier standing several feet away, watching her. He was an older man, with gray replacing the bronze at his temples and forehead, and he had a kind, weathered face. He held his weapon loosely in front of him, smiling at her. She returned the smile and decided she could leave the protection of her people to him and his men. The weight of her long hours had settled onto her eyelids. A few hours remained until breakfast would be served and she hadn't had much sleep. She moved toward her own bed for a brief nap, the calm she'd sought finally filling her.

CHAPTER EIGHTEEN

Hawk marched into the civilian cafeteria at the head of a double line of twenty-four soldiers. Williams marched beside her, decked out in full battle gear, his gloved hands wrapped loosely around his M4A1 Carbine assault rifle. He was at ease, as were his men, but Hawk had something of a sixth sense about operations. She smelled blood in the air and knew lives would be lost today. She couldn't be certain whether those lives would be her men or the enemy. She had chosen her best soldiers. They were bright and fast and they were good. Probably as good as the United States Army had.

She spoke to Williams without looking at him, her words falling in cadence with the boots all around her. "Quick in, quick out, minimal engagement, understood? You smell shit you pull back on the double."

"Yes, ma'am."

She stopped and turned to him, catching the tail end of a smile before he turned to her and saluted. She held her salute for the blink of an eye before sending him on his way past the tables and into the kitchen. None of the soldiers broke formation to look at her as they hurried past, but she took in every face. She had enough engraved wrist bands at home to make her value every man and woman in her company. Her name would have been on one several times over if not for them. She did not want to add to her collection. She didn't want to mourn another soldier with a cold strip of metal.

A voice spoke behind her. "What's going on, Major Hawk?"

She waited until the last of the soldiers had gone by before turning and answering.

"Good morning again, Ms. Moore." Several of the civilians looked up from their eggs and toast. Those who could overhear pretended not to be listening, but the movement of their forks became slow and mechanical. Hawk motioned for Gail to follow her out of earshot.

"We noted a potential entry point when reviewing schematics last night. A maintenance passage we can use to get through to the prisoner's side of the complex."

"A maintenance passage? But they should all be sealed."

Hawk moved to a beverage station and poured herself a mug of black coffee, and continued in a hushed voice. "This one appears to not have the same airtight seals as the others. The kitchens for the prisoners' wing and the corporate wing are right next to each other—they share a wall."

"Right, but there is only a single connection between them." Gail pointed across the cafeteria at the dark hallway that was blocked several yards on by the airlock door and then by the barricade a few feet beyond that. "Where is this passage you found?"

Hawk sipped her coffee, her thoughts with the sound of boots diminishing in the kitchen behind her. "Beneath each kitchen are several floors of food prep and storage. The lowest floor is three flights down and contains a pair of walk-in refrigerators and freezers. Between the two and stretching through the blast wall that separates the wings is an open space that allows for repair access to the walk-ins."

A small group of civilians wandered to the end of the nearest cafeteria table, striking up a half-hearted conversation with the two women seated there.

"Passage may be too grand a word for it, more like a crawl space. I'm not entirely sure the designers even intended for the two areas to be linked. But the bottom line is that my men can access the space through a panel in the refrigerator on this side and get through to the refrigerator on their side. They only have to cut through the panel over there, but, like I said, it's several floors down so the prisoners won't be able to hear."

More workers ambled over to the nearby table and Hawk led Gail further away. One of the women rolled her eyes at the newcomers and scooped up her tray, walking past Gail and Hawk on her way to the dishwasher. Gail didn't seem to notice the growing crowd. She poured hot water into a mug and dropped in a tea bag, bobbing it up and down in the steaming water, her eyes unfocused as her mind worked.

"Will they be able to overpower the prisoners? There didn't seem to be many of your team."

"That's not their mission." Hawk put down her empty mug and moved to the door, Gail following a few steps behind. "They'll make their way quietly to the manual airlock controls and pop the door for us. I have another two platoons en route here to be in place when the door goes up. We'll storm the cafeteria and take them down with minimum casualties. My hope is that they'll surrender when they see so many soldiers bearing down on them. If not...well, there are only a handful of guns in there and we'll have the team from downstairs coming up from behind. If we have to engage it should be quick."

Hawk stopped at the door and turned. The movement was so abrupt that Gail bumped into her, the tight hold of her pencil skirt nearly toppling her over. Hawk reached out and put a hand around her waist, steadying the woman against her body. She felt Gail stiffen at the firm grip of her arm. Hawk stilled on the edge of saying something, her lips parted an inch and her eyes steady on Gail's. The woman who'd dropped off her tray slipped past them again on her way out of the cafeteria. The movement in her peripheral vision snapped Hawk's daze. She let go quickly. Gail's heels hit the floor with a click, and it wasn't until she heard the sound that Hawk realized Gail had been standing on her toes.

The sound of boots came from behind them. Hawk cleared her throat as the first of the soldiers came level with them and said, "My men will be clearing the civilians out of the cafeteria. It may be a good idea for you to be back in there to reassure them."

Gail nodded with a detachment that surprised Hawk and made her way back to the tables. Perhaps her proximity to the battle yesterday had shaken her. She hadn't been this compliant before.

Within a few minutes, the room was clear of noncombatants. Hawk followed behind them on her way to the Command Center. Williams's team was in place when she arrived.

This is Williams reporting in. Do you read me, Major?

Loud and clear, Captain. Good to hear from you. We picked up video from your body camera a few minutes ago but we were deaf up here. I was worried the mics wouldn't come through all the steel and concrete.

Just a busted unit, ma'am. Got it switched out while we were cutting through the panel on the prisoner side. Can you see the entry point?

I can. Looks like a neat punch through.

Just like we planned. My team's ready to move out with your word.

Go ahead, Williams, but keep your eyes peeled for resistance.

Yes, ma'am.

The camera swayed drunkenly as he crawled forward on his belly through the narrow space. Hawk focused on the blurry image of the light spilling through a four-foot-square hole in the ceiling of the refrigerator on the prisoners' side. A pair of soldiers with hissing blowtorches was stowing their gear at the edges of the screen, the flame glowing painfully in the modified night vision of the camera.

Hawk sat back in her chair and looked around. For their safety during the assault, Hawk had decided to bring all of the civilians to The Docks where they could be guarded by her soldiers if things went south on the other side of the compound. She had opened the front of her Command Center so that she could watch the feed and talk to Williams while also keeping an eye on the state of the civilians. She watched them milling around, arms hugged closed around their stomachs, clinging together in small groups and talking little.

We're in place at the walk-in door.

Hawk's eyes snapped back to the screen, where a final pair of camouflaged legs was dropping to the ground amidst stacked boxes of produce.

Waiting for your word, Major.

That nagging doubt crept back into Hawk's mind, and she pushed it aside as she had a dozen times before. The burden of command.

Proceed when ready, Captain.

The refrigerator door pushed open and, led by Williams, the group spilled out into the prisoners' pantry. He had taken less than a dozen steps, his eyes and weapon sweeping in arcs as he proceeded, when everything went wrong. This room should have been empty. The prisoners should have been lazing around upstairs. Instead, the speakers crackled with the muffled pops of gunfire. There was shouting, both from far away and close to the microphone, and the incessant rattle of machine gun fire.

Right flank! Right flank!

The camera spun and dropped, Williams's knee on the concrete floor visible for a flash before the camera was looking along the barrel of his weapon and every other sound was swallowed by the roar of bullets from his M4. Empty shells zipped across the screen as the weapon spoke in staccato bursts. Hawk's heart rate picked up, but she sat still and watched, knowing better than to shout questions into Williams's ear during a firefight.

People started crowding around the monitor. Hawk watched the screen intently, focusing on the broken images and the intermittent voices. For a moment she thought she recognized one of the prisoners. A man with a long black ponytail and a collar of tattoos. His teeth were clenched as he fired endlessly from his hip as though he was starring in an action movie rather than fighting for his life. Williams's weapon turned to him and his chest opened up, blooming like a red rose over his heart.

The prisoner wasn't the only one hit. Between shots Hawk could hear screaming in a half dozen different pitches, and it was clear who had the upper hand. The prisoners had benefited from the element of surprise, but they also had a far superior position with better cover and the enemy in a bottleneck. The camera suddenly shuddered as if caught in a stiff wind, and there was a loud grunt in the microphone.

Fall back! Everyone fall back!

There was an edge to Williams's voice that Hawk knew well. Her jaw clenched. He tried to stand, but the screen wavered again and he was back on one knee, his breathing loud and labored in the speakers.

Williams

I'm fine. Fall back!

Williams

The scene was still and silent. Hawk felt the people around her closing in. Williams took a few long breaths.

On your feet, soldier!

The camera moved so quickly it made her slightly queasy. Williams fired a few wild shots, his left arm unable to support the barrel of his weapon. He staggered back, slumping against an obstruction. The next burst of gunfire was followed by an unearthly scream. The camera crashed to the ground, hovering inches off the gray concrete. It rose and fell a couple of times before a pair of sand-brown boots came into view. Gunfire rattled around them as the camera was dragged across the floor, a streak of red painted behind it like the tail of a comet. It stopped, facing another set of fatigues, torn flesh and wasted bone peeking through the fabric.

Major? Major are you there? This is Pearson.

The woman's voice was strained, but not frantic, and Hawk spoke in even tones to keep it that way.

I'm here, Sergeant. Report.

Five casualties, ma'am. I counted maybe six or seven on the other side. Hard to tell. We've pulled back to the walk-in and we're barricading the door to cover our retreat.

Will you be able to evac the injured through that panel?

Yes, ma'am. We'll manage. Wouldn't say no to a friendly hand or two to help out if they can be spared.

Hawk snapped the fingers on her right hand and one of her men immediately dialed into his headset.

They're on the way right now, Sergeant. Get the injured to the Clinic and I'll meet you there in five.

Yes, ma'am.

Hawk stood very slowly and smoothed her uniform jacket. The tent around her was silent, despite the crush of bodies. She reached for the headset and clawed it from her ear, throwing it at the tabletop in disgust. Gail, standing nearby, jumped at the sound of the plastic cracking. She squeaked in surprise and Hawk's eyes were on her in an instant. Then they slid off her again as a movement caught Hawk's eye.

A bright-red ponytail whipped around and its owner disappeared in the crowd. Something about the sight caught in her memory, and it didn't take long for her to remember the woman with the tray in the cafeteria. She had walked by twice during Hawk's conversation with Gail. How much had she heard? It seemed odd that she would have been so near so often. Now, when all the other civilians apart from Gail were gathered as far as possible from the scene of action, she was nearby again. It was too much of a coincidence.

Hawk started walking and her men parted to let her pass. Her hand wrapped around Gail's upper arm in a firm but not bruising grip. "Come with me."

The red ponytail was easy to spot. She was weaving through the crowd, moving steadily away from the tents even as the others were pressing forward to find out what was happening. The redhead turned and looked over her shoulder as the crowd thinned, and her eyes met Hawk's. That was the moment Hawk knew she was right. Fear was palpable in her look, and she picked up her pace, almost running. The soldier's measured strides outpaced the woman. With each step she got closer, and with each step she was surer of her next move.

When she was within a few feet of the woman she dropped Gail's arm and raised her sidearm in one smooth motion. "That's far enough."

CHAPTER NINETEEN

Hawk focused on an even, steady pace as she walked through the corridor toward the civilian housing block. Each time she passed one of her soldiers, she returned their salute, meeting every pair of eyes. She'd intended to do the same with civilians so they could gain strength through her confidence, but there were no civilians in the corridors. They were all tucked away in their rooms out of either exhaustion or fear. She couldn't really blame them. The situation was rather bleak at the moment even for her.

The problem she faced, of course, given this second betrayal, was how many more people in this station were under Red's sway. It had been unforgivably foolhardy to discuss her plans in such an open environment as the cafeteria, and now her men had paid the price for it. Her only excuse was that she had no reason to believe any of the civilians would have put their own lives at risk. That was a ridiculous assumption, particularly considering Hawk had ample evidence that humans rarely acted in their own best interests. It had occurred to her that the safest course was to put the entire station on lockdown, but she wanted to speak to the secretary before she made that move. She doubted they would react favorably to being detained and she couldn't afford a second rebellion.

Turning the corner, lost in her thoughts, Hawk found her way blocked. Gail stood immobile in the center of the hall, staring silently into the distance. Hawk took a self-indulgent moment to inspect the long, gleaming trail of her hair and athletic lines of her body. It was a memorable body, one that would have garnered far more of her attention in a more appropriate setting. When Gail didn't react to her presence, Hawk to another step forward.

"Administrator Moore?"

At the sound of her name, she jumped, spinning on the spot and dropping into a defensive position. Out of instinct, Hawk mimicked the action, only holding out raised palms rather than fists to show she was no threat.

"Whoa. Sorry to startle you. Everything's okay."

Gail let out a low breath and stood a little straighter, but the tension didn't leave her. She still looked as though she might lash out at any moment. More than that, there was something distinctly wrong in Gail's manner. That appealing confidence she'd exuded not so long ago was all but gone. There was a hollowness to her gaze. Perhaps it was fatigue, it had after all, been a very long, trying day, but Hawk guessed there was something deeper going on.

"What's wrong? What happened?"

A detailed response seemed imminent, but then Gail's gaze hardened. She laughed, but there was defeat rather than joy in the sound. She reached out with a shaking hand, pressing Hawk's arm down with gentle pressure. "Nothing, Major Hawk. You frightened me is all."

At the touch of Gail's fingers on her bare forearm, warmth spread across Hawk's skin and up into her chest. Her touch was soft where everything else in Hawk's life of late had been hard and coarse. Loneliness made her want to prolong the contact, but she had a duty to the uniform she wore and so she let her arm fall, separating from Gail's touch. Maybe she imagined the way Gail's fingertips lingered on her skin or the flash of interest in her look. A hopeful part of her considered the possibilities when all this was over, but she knew how dangerous thoughts like that could be.

"I imagine you've come to question Beatrice," Gail said in a voice as flat as her eyes.

"She can wait." Hawk crossed her arms, leveling a challenging look at Gail. "I need to know you're with me. Why don't you tell me what's on your mind? We don't have time for games."

Fiery anger sparked in Gail's gaze, then flickered out. She turned away as she spoke, "We don't have time, do we? Not anymore. Our options have run out."

"Not quite yet."

"There was so much time and I wasted it. Three long years and I've wasted every day."

"What do you mean?"

"Three years is long enough for me to get to know fifty men," she said, leaning heavily on the wall. "But I didn't. I've been standing here thinking about it and I don't really know more than half of them. I never took the time to get to know my people."

"You know all of the civilians here. Every one of them and they love you for it."

"But I know none of the prisoners and they hate me for it. Don't you see? I've failed them. They're just as much my people as the civilians are but I never treated them like it. And not all of the civilians love me."

"Drumm doesn't…"

"Not Drumm," Gail said, nodding down the hall. "Beatrice didn't love me. She did what I couldn't. See saw them as people, not prisoners. Not two populations, just one."

"You see how well that worked out for her. A prisoner in her own room, responsible for the deaths of my men and the danger to both civilians and prisoners."

"No, Major Hawk. I'm responsible for that."

For a heart-stopping moment Hawk worried that she was about to hear the confession of another traitor. She dismissed the idea as soon as it came. This woman could never be seduced by Red. She had too much courage and too much intelligence to be his victim. She was, however, uniquely capable of being a victim to her own guilt.

"I'm responsible for Beatrice's actions." Gail continued and the more she spoke, the more life flooded out of her. "I'm responsible for Red's actions. I'm responsible because I let my prejudice show me criminals rather than men."

Pity stole over Hawk so heavily she couldn't speak. She knew Gail was wrong, she was letting hopelessness get the better of her because she carried the weight of too much responsibility. The thought made her angry, not at Gail or even Red, but at Andrus for putting her here with no support. Her anger and her pity kept her silent for too long. She saw the way Gail's body shrunk in the face of that silence. She thought Hawk agreed with her.

"If Andrus had wanted unity up here they shouldn't have made such a clear separation," Hawk argued too late. "They gave you an impossible tightrope to walk."

Gail stood straighter and smoothed the lapels of her blazer. "I'm certain you don't blame the Army for any failed missions, I won't blame Andrus for mine. What is the next move, Major Hawk?"

The abrupt shift left Hawk unsettled, and she had no choice but honesty. "I don't know yet." She looked around the deserted corridor, acutely aware of previous indiscretions in discussing strategy. "I need to consult my team."

"Sounds like you've run out of options."

"Not exactly. We've had several setbacks." Hawk grimaced at her lack of conviction. "And I won't pretend our options are unlimited, but we will win this. We just need time to regroup and rest. Everything will come together in the morning."

Gail didn't respond. There was so little to say. She nodded and walked away from Hawk, a shell of the leader and woman she had been. It was clear that Hawk hadn't convinced her. If anything, she'd made everything worse. There was more to be said, but it would have to wait.

With a frustrated sigh, Hawk headed down the corridor toward her interview with the second traitor.

CHAPTER TWENTY

Hawk thought about commandeering an office or perhaps a storage room for the interrogation. Something austere and cold to make her subject feel out of place. Make her feel alone and scared. That was a CIA technique Hawk had used to question suspected terrorists detained in her various missions.

But this time, Hawk went in a completely different direction. She had the woman sent back to her own apartment, followed by three soldiers, but led by three members of the security personnel. She would have to stare at men she worked with every day as she walked. She would think about how she'd betrayed them.

Hawk had an inkling that she may not respond to fear, but she'd almost certainly respond to guilt. When she'd been caught she'd looked at Gail with what appeared genuine remorse. Hawk would probably never know how Red got to her, but, whatever his approach, the woman knew what she'd done was wrong. If Hawk could tap into her shame over that, she might just turn this disaster into an advantage.

After giving her time to stew alone in her room, Hawk finally met their newest traitor. Just as Hawk had predicted, she was a mess. She sat on the couch, her knees pulled up to her chest and her head down, ignoring the soldiers standing around her. The young woman didn't flinch when Hawk sent the others away—she just sat still and quiet.

Andrus obviously hadn't put a lot of thought into the staff living quarters. This particular room was all beige walls, plum carpet and glass-topped tables. The wall conformed to the curve of the dome and the furniture was bubbly and curvy to match. Porthole windows over the couch gave a view of black sky and pinprick stars. A single door led off to one side and the whole place wasn't much larger than a dorm room. The design was familiar and, as she sat on one of the plush chairs in front of the couch, Hawk realized why. The room was an exact copy of the living quarters in *Star Trek: The Next Generation*, one of Hawk's favorites as a teen. Maybe the designers had a little imagination after all.

"What's your name?"

The redhead didn't reply. Hawk knew the answer, having discussed it with Gail, but she was determined to get this girl talking.

"I said, what's your name?"

Still nothing.

"Hey!" Hawk clapped, a sharp, loud noise that echoed in the small room.

The girl jumped, her head snapping up to show sad, wet eyes. "Beatrice."

That was a start. It was the truth at the very least. Beatrice Jane Melton. Executive Secretary for Administrator Gail Moore, Andrus Industries, Moon Base. Twenty-four years old from Hereford, Texas. Moved to New York City at age nineteen. Working for Andrus since age twenty.

"How did you tip him off, Beatrice? How'd you tell him about the attack?"

"I didn't."

Hawk let the words sit in the air. They hadn't been uttered with much conviction. She'd been caught out and she knew it. Eventually, Beatrice's cheeks turned pink and she looked away, unable to maintain eye contact with Hawk.

"How did you contact him?"

Rather than answer, Beatrice stood up and crossed to the open door. Hawk followed her into a small bedroom and watched her shuffle through a drawer of lacy underwear. She held out a palm-sized electronic device and shuffled back to the couch.

Hawk had seen something like this on the belt of the station security guards. It could have been a smart phone, but it didn't have a speaker. From what she could gather, it was similar to an old-fashioned pager, designed to send text messages from one device to another without access to the main computer network. When she tried to power it on, however, the screen stayed black.

"The battery's not dead," Beatrice said, curling herself back into a ball. "I made sure to charge it. It just doesn't work anymore. I don't know why."

Hawk did. An hour ago a new stage of the battery preservation schedule went into effect. All communication devices within the compound were down. Even more lighting would go in twelve hours or so. Then elevators in another twelve. From there it would be hard to stop the inevitable. She had a hunch the device wouldn't have worked even if the telecom system was still up. Red wouldn't leave this loose end around. Not when it had already served its purpose.

"Did Stone have one of these, too?"

Beatrice bristled, spitting out her response with obvious distaste. "Of course not. I'm the only one who had one."

"His communication with Red was funneled through you, wasn't it?" Beatrice bottled up at the question, but the answer was obvious. "Communications with civilians isn't monitored. Red was clearly in touch with Stone. Did that go through you? What was it—emails? Paper letters? Calls?"

She remained obstinately silent, so Hawk pushed a little harder. "If it wasn't through you he must have trusted someone else up here with his mail."

"He trusts me more than anyone!"

"But he does trust someone else up here?"

Her fishing attempts were empty again. Beatrice clammed up, looking out the window rather that engaging. Hawk tried to read her body language. Her gut told her that there were no more traitors, but she couldn't trust her gut. She'd have to lock them all down after all. She did the math in her head. Between the soldiers at the Clinic to guard Stone, the team at the refrigerator and the guards she'd need to post outside this room, the strength available to storm the prisoner side was dwindling. Their chances of success rose exponentially with an overwhelming attack force. She didn't want to spare the men to guard people who would probably turn out to be innocent. She needed to break Beatrice.

"What did he promise you?" Hawk asked, placing the useless device on the table between them.

Beatrice didn't answer. She started to cry.

"Did he tell you no one would die?"

The tears came harder, her body perfectly still as they slid down her smooth cheeks.

"Did he promise to protect you?"

She buried her head in her knees again.

"He lied to you, Beatrice. He lied to you and he's going to watch you die just like the rest of us."

"No!" There was strength in her shout, but the tears hadn't stopped. They coated her words and made them harder to understand. "No one's going to die. He's not like that! He's a kind man. A good man."

"A good man serving two consecutive life sentences?"

It was a bluff, but Beatrice wouldn't have believed Red capable of any crime, even if Hawk had known what it was. Her tears were slowing now and she was starting to show life. "That's a lie. He's innocent. He told me everything."

"And you believe him?"

"He wouldn't lie to me. He's a good man. A loving man."

Now they were getting somewhere. Hawk didn't need reality from this conversation, she just needed to know Beatrice's reality. She needed to know what this girl thought Red's motives were because he had to have told her a version of the truth. The best liars mix their lies with truth and use that to force their way into other's confidence.

"Then why is he asking you to hurt your friends? Would a good man do that?"

"I'm not hurting my friends. I'm only hurting you. The people sent up here to kill him."

"We weren't sent to…"

"You can't trick me. I heard him! He said that was the plan!"

"Who?"

"Michael Richards, CEO Compton's assistant." Beatrice dropped her feet to the floor and sat up straighter. "I heard him talking to Ms. Moore. I heard him say they'd ordered you to kill the prisoners. Kill Red. I won't let you do it!"

Of course she'd heard that. That was why he went after Beatrice in the first place. She had access to Gail and so she had access to everything. How many other conversations had she been witness to? How many messages had she intercepted and sent along to Red?

"Ms. Moore trusted you." Hawk spoke with as much sadness as she could muster. She felt only anger, but she needed to make Beatrice feel her betrayal. "She still trusts you."

Her tears came with a vengeance. Whatever this woman had done, there was at least one person on this side of the barricade she cared about. Unfortunately, it was the person she'd hurt the most.

"You won't tell her will you? Please don't tell her. I didn't mean to listen. I never meant to…"

"She knows. Of course she knows." It was time to go for the kill, but Hawk still hesitated. "She's probably always suspected, but she cared about you too much to think you would do this."

Beatrice wailed. It was a plaintive sound. It would've broken Hawk's heart in any other circumstance. Right now, however, she struggled to contain her anger at the whimpering, sniveling idiot in front of her. Three of her soldiers were dead. Williams hadn't yet regained consciousness. The two platoons originally tasked with storming the cafeteria were now guarding the refrigerator's vulnerable point instead of patrolling the base. Time was running out and options were running out even faster. But this girl was worried her boss would be mad at her.

"Tell me what he's planning, Beatrice. You owe that to Ms. Moore."

She knew immediately that she'd overstepped. The girl's face twisted and Hawk realized that she hadn't been crying about Gail.

"I'll never betray him. Never. He loves me."

CHAPTER TWENTY-ONE

The corporate housing block of Moon Base was topped by three floors of offices. They were set up not unlike your average regional headquarters of any Earth-bound corporation—padded cubicles, the lingering smell of warm inkjet toner, motivational posters on the walls and the hum of various electronics. If it weren't for the fact that they were two hundred and thirty-nine thousand miles from the closest Starbucks, most of the workers would hardly realize they were on the Moon. The main floors had no exterior windows, despite the fact that they were so close to the dome.

The top floor, however, held the largest, most opulent office and had a wall of windows overlooking the desolate landscape. The office of the Facility Administrator. The CEO of the Moon as her employees called her. On the days when they faced the Sun, this room was warm and bright and full of energy. Tonight, however, with the long lunar night only forty-eight hours old and the life-giving batteries slowly but inexorably dying, there was little life in the room.

Gail sat in her high-backed leather chair looking out over the landscape. She rarely did so, her focus usually on her computer or her telephone. Both of those distractions were as dead as the rocks littering the ground outside, and so she indulged herself in the view dimly illuminated by the glow from the dome. A tumbler half full of amber liquid rested on one arm of the chair, cradled in her loose grip. Another rare indulgence she felt she had earned. Gray smoke coiled around her dark hair as she took another long drag from her cigarette. All of her vices were showing themselves tonight, and she grinned darkly at her greed.

She ignored a knock at the door. After a decent pause the knock came again and again, but she ignored the summons, instead focusing on her scotch and cigarette. The door opened and Gail knew who it was even without the reflection in the window.

* * *

"Administrator Moore?"

She took a slow sip of scotch and stared through the window. "Call me Gail."

Hawk cleared her throat and took a step closer to the desk, gripping her hands behind her back. "The young lady confessed to alerting the prisoners of the attack."

"Beatrice." She tapped her cigarette with a rounded fingernail. Hawk watched white flecks float from the tip into the ashtray below allowing the end to glow a little brighter. "She was my secretary. You passed her desk on the way in here. She's worked for me since we began operations three years ago. She special-ordered my favorite perfume to be sent up for my birthday two months ago."

Hawk shuffled her feet, unsure what to do with the information.

"It probably cost her a week's pay. And she is well paid, I assure you." Gail gestured with her glass toward the glowing dome in the distance to her right. "She used to go visit the cows. We have a herd down there. She said it reminded her of her father's ranch in Texas." She emptied the glass and stubbed out her cigarette. "Said that she felt at home there among the animals."

Hawk crossed her arms over her chest and studied the back of the chair. "She said the same thing Stone said. He loves me. I'm not sure when he got to her, but she's going to stay locked up until this is over."

Gail crossed to the cabinet to her right. She took another tumbler along with a tall, square bottle with a blue tint to the glass. She filled the two glasses high enough to cause Hawk's eyebrow to shoot up before returning to the desk and holding out the second glass. Hawk hesitated for a moment, but gave in to the hard look leveled at her.

Gail gestured to the chair across the desk. Hawk took a sip, enjoying the peppery heat that flowed across her tongue and scorched her throat.

"This is excellent." She sat on the edge of the chair and cradled the glass in her fingers. "What are we drinking to?"

Gail pressed another cigarette between her lips and lit it. "The end of the world?"

"Not quite yet."

"Cigarette?"

"I quit."

"Me too." She lounged back in her chair and the shoulders of her blazer bunched around her cream silk blouse. "Beatrice keeps a carton in her desk."

Hawk took another long sip, the peaty flavor filling her nostrils. "When we spoke earlier you seemed…"

"I don't want to talk about that."

"Fair enough." The whiskey started to buzz through her thoughts and it was a struggle to keep her eyes up, away from the top button straining against the pull of Gail's silk blouse. "What would you like to talk about?"

Perhaps it was a trick of the low, emergency lighting that made Gail's eyes shine. Her gaze flickered to the solitary picture frame on her desk. "Do you have a family, Major Hawk?"

"I do. One hundred six strong."

Smoke trickled from Gail's nostrils. "I don't mean your men."

"I know what you mean." She was surprised to find her glass empty, and even more surprised to find herself walking to the cabinet and bringing the bottle back. "I had a brother who died in a car accident in high school and both my parents are gone."

"Never married?"

Warning bells that she hadn't heard in a long time went off as she shook her head. Gail's eyes went back to the picture frame, but they were definitely dry. When Hawk leaned over to refill her glass she shot a sideways glance at it, but the angle was wrong. "You?"

Gail took a long time answering, her eyes locked on the frame. Finally she said in a voice so quiet it was almost swallowed by the empty room, "She won't miss me."

Something seemed to be stealing Hawk's breath away. All she could do was wait and watch. Gail finally looked at her, and there was something so raw and yet so distant in her gaze that Hawk gripped the chair hard to keep herself from falling into those eyes. She turned the picture frame, and Hawk tore her eyes away with difficulty from the haunting face.

The air came back into her lungs at the sight of the photograph. A little girl, maybe seven or eight years old, smiling at the camera with a wide-open grin. She was missing two teeth, but the rest were tiny and perfectly straight. Her hair was raven black in pigtails and she had freckles on her big, round cheeks. Her face filled the frame and Hawk found herself smiling along with the little girl for no particular reason other than it felt right.

"Lou-Lou." Gail turned the frame back to look at the smile that didn't touch her. "She was my daughter."

"Was?"

"I lost her." She stubbed out her cigarette and put the frame back in its place, adjusting it to the exact angle it had been at before and then laying her palms flat on the wooden surface. "Not like that. She's alive. *She* isn't lost. She's just lost to *me*. I don't think that makes sense."

Hawk smiled and laughed a little. "Not exactly, no."

It struck Gail that she had not seen the woman smile since she'd arrived on Moon Base. Not even a polite, disinterested turn of the lips. This was wide and open and utterly breathtaking. She had to look down at her fingers, splayed out across the polished cherry wood and search for her next thought.

"I met her mother at Brown. She was an artist and so... open. Like she had nothing to hide from the world. I saw one of her paintings in the student gallery and stared at it for hours. It was elegant and effortless and at the time..." Lingering smoke caught her attention for a moment and she watched it flutter in the air disturbed by her breath and yet she did not appear to see it at all. "She walked up to me and smiled and I knew everything there was to know about her in that moment. She was everything that I wasn't and, to a nineteen-year-old girl from the Rez, that seemed like a good thing."

Bitter regret washed across her face and Hawk remembered what it was to be nineteen. To be a girl who thought she was a woman, but was really just a fool. Gail left her eyes on the ashtray as she continued, "Andrus recruited me out of college. They saw my potential and I was thrilled to have the chance to prove myself. Angelique came with me to New York and we set up in Manhattan, living the life we had both always wanted. I was an up-and-comer at a major corporation, and she was a Manhattan socialite with our apartment full of genteel paintings she would titter about and sell to her friends."

"But something changed."

"No, actually. That's the funny thing. Nothing changed. She loved me. She always had." She took a moment to let the scotch trickle down her throat and burn some of the regret away. "I loved to work. I always had. I would work late and not call. When I got home she would be crying and we would fight. God how we fought. She kept pulling me closer, and I...I should have tried, I suppose. She deserved better."

A well of sadness opened up in Hawk, and she had to look away. The words echoed inside her, but in her own voice, spoken countless times and with varying levels of pain attached to them.

How many times had she felt that regret and told herself it had been the right thing to do?

"She had the idea that Lou-Lou would bring me home. A child would wake something in me and repair our relationship."

This time when Gail reached for a cigarette Hawk picked up the lighter and lit one for both of them. The first deep breath of smoke burned more than the scotch, but the way it made her head reel was worth the pain.

"That seems to be a popularly held delusion. That a child will fix a broken relationship. I love my daughter with all of my heart, but I loved Angelique with all of my heart as well. Apparently, my heart is not very big. All that I had to give wasn't enough for them and she found enough in another Wall Street Widow. It wasn't until I moved out of our chic Manhattan apartment to make way for her new love that it occurred to me I hadn't really tried that hard. Still, she made sure I was a part of Lou-Lou's life. She's certainly a better woman than me."

The silence in the room echoed for a long time, Hawk rolling the cigarette between her thumb and middle finger and Gail openly watching her.

"I apologize. I shouldn't have shared so much. My burden has made you uncomfortable."

Hawk inhaled hard, the tobacco burning right down to the filter before she put it out. "No, you haven't made me uncomfortable. I was just thinking."

Gail forced her voice to a falsely cheery, teasing tone. "I'm guessing there are a string of scorned lovers crying their eyes out at your absence tonight. You strike me as a heartbreaker."

"No, not a heartbreaker. Not on purpose, anyway. No string of lovers. No great lost love. Not really much to speak of at all."

"I find that hard to believe, Major Hawk."

"Please," she said, looking at Gail through her lashes. "Call me Charlie."

She tried out the name on her tongue and found that she enjoyed the taste. "Charlie."

Hawk didn't even try to hide her interest, watching Gail's lips moving. "Soldiers have a reputation we don't all deserve.

I'm not the type to pick up random women in bars or start dead-end relationships at each deployment."

"No one at all worth speaking of?"

She shrugged and ran a hand through her hair. "I'm not a nun or anything, it's just…" She propped her ankle on her knee and fiddled with the fabric of her pants while she tried to find the words. "When I joined the Army I signed a piece of paper that said I wouldn't give them anything to ask about. I stand by my word, so I haven't had much of anything to tell."

"Don't Ask, Don't Tell ended a long time ago, Charlie."

"Once you get into a habit, it can be a hard thing to break."

Gail stood, peeling her blazer off and dropping it onto her chair as she moved around the desk. The silk blouse was sleeveless, showing off the smooth, olive skin of her slim arms. She leaned back on the corner of the desk, her long leg brushing intoxicatingly close to Hawk, who froze as the warmth of Gail's body came so close but so agonizingly far. She rested her weight back on her arms, the straight line of her skirt riding up to mid-thigh. Hawk watched the hem waver and then hold, the promise of what was underneath making her ache in the pit of her stomach.

Gail raised the glass to her lips slowly enough to prove it was on purpose. Her eyes locked on Hawk's and did not move as she tipped the glass back and emptied it. Her neck was long and graceful as the rest of her, and the skin there was just slightly flushed. She set the empty glass deliberately in the very center of the polished top of the desk.

"How very disciplined of you, Major Hawk."

She dragged the title out indecently, her lips wrapping around the syllables. Hawk felt a surge of desire and the alarm bells that had gone off before were now a cacophony in her ears. Or perhaps that was the pounding of blood through her body at the thought of those lips. Of the tongue that shaped the words. She dropped her foot back to the ground and stood, her stillness suddenly unbearable, as though the gravity of the room had tripled.

"I should be going. Thank you for the drink."

She turned to head for the door, but Gail's hands were on her in a flash, grabbing fistfuls of her uniform jacket and pulling her in. She let herself be pulled, dragged into the orbit of this coldly alluring woman. Gail slid back onto the desk, steering Hawk between her legs. Gail's hand was on the back of her neck, pulling her roughly into a hard kiss that involved as much teeth as tongue and lips. Hawk's body responded even when her mind was slow to catch up, kissing back eagerly and wrapping her hands around Gail's slim waist.

The kiss stretched on and deepened. Hawk's mind spun with the mingled taste of scotch, tobacco, and lust. Gail's hands danced across her body, barely fumbling as she slid the jacket from her shoulders, massaging the muscles now clad in a tight, sand-colored T-shirt.

She broke the kiss and panted. "Gail." But was pulled back in before any other words escaped.

The movement pushed the skirt up Gail's thighs, and their bodies met, sending a burst of pleasure through them both and earning a groan from Hawk that was swallowed in the rejoined kiss. Gail managed to get the jacket off her arms, and she grabbed Hawk's hand, moving it to her own breast and gasping at the feel of the calloused thumb rubbing across silk and lace.

"We can't…"

Gail cupped her face between her hands and looked into Hawk's eyes. This close, Hawk could make out individual flecks of gold among the amber and the flare of green at the center of her irises. The look in them, though, was the part she could not quite get past. There was lust, to be sure, but her eyes were ice. The fire of her desire burned, but it burned cold and hard. There was no affection, no hint of softness, just need. Powerful and raw as a fresh wound and so very vulnerable.

"I haven't felt anything in so long, Hawk." She tore her shirt open and popped open the lace bra, letting it fall. Her breasts were perfectly round and heaving with every shuddering breath. She took Hawk's hands in her own, guiding them to replace the discarded garment and rolling her eyes at the touch.

"Please." She leaned in, her lips stopping just far enough away to brush Hawk's. "Please make me feel something."

The agony of the request and the way it mirrored her own need slashed through Hawk like a physical blow. She surged forward, capturing those lips in a bruising kiss. Gail wrapped around her. Softness enveloped her in a way completely foreign to her hard, ordered world. Her hips ground forward of their own accord, finding the friction she craved as much against the cold edge of the desk as the woman before her.

Soon her eagerness could not be contained and she wrapped an arm around Gail's waist, lifting her far enough off the surface to slide the skirt out of her way and slip the woman's panties down. She dropped her back onto the desk and moved back into the shelter of her legs.

"God, yes. Please, Charlie…please touch me."

She did not need a second invitation. Hawk trailed the tips of her fingers up the creamy flesh of Gail's thigh, watching their progress with hungry eyes. Gail trembled in her arms, her breath low and fevered. Hawk felt a flush of pride at the effect her attentions were having, but it was short-lived, knowing that her own response was just as strong.

As though reading her mind, Gail attacked the buttons of Hawk's pants, determined to get through the many layers of clothing as quickly as she could. Then Hawk's fingers found home and Gail's touch faltered with a moan of pleasure. The sound sent a shockwave of need through Hawk. Perhaps she had been more desperate for this than she thought. Gail responded to her slightest touch like a woman on the brink of starvation. If her wild eyes were any indicator, maybe she was on the brink. Hawk moved more eagerly than she would have liked, but she knew they both needed wildness now. Gail shouted at the touch and her hips bucked forward.

To their mutual surprise, Gail's body jerked and shuddered as release ripped through her. It was everything Hawk could do to hold on as Gail screamed and tore long gashes down her back through the T-shirt. She grunted with the pain of it, but the throb between her legs intensified to a dizzying degree.

Just as Gail's screams subsided, Hawk began again, earning a startled change in pitch to the scream of her name. Gail pulled her into a kiss, rocking her hips to match Hawk's punishing rhythm. Their bodies moved together like the sea, waves of pleasure coursing through both with every pass.

They moved together in a dance lacking in grace but drenched in desire. Sounds that she did not recognize burst past Hawk's lips. They were feral, primal sounds that were mirrored by those panted in her ear. She rose on a wave of pleasure. Her body shivered with mingled heat and cold, her nerves on fire. Just when she thought she could not hold back her own release for another moment, Gail's teeth clamped down on her neck right at her pulse point and roared with pleasure into the trapped flesh. The bite was what threw her over the edge, and she rammed her body forward one final time before her sight was lost in popping white lights and every muscle in her body locked and then exploded. She screamed to the heavens that felt so close here in the emptiness of space and then collapsed, her body drenched in sweat, her lungs crying out for air.

As her senses returned, she noticed the trembling beneath her had changed. Gail wrapped her arms tightly around Hawk's shoulders, pulling her in as tears spilled down her neck. She could not quite process the change or the overt show of emotion from this woman who had been so calm and so reserved. She stroked the long, black hair with her free hand and the tears only came faster, the grip on her shoulders painfully hard.

"I'm not going to let you die here."

Gail's tears stopped abruptly, her body went rigid. She pulled away from Hawk's body and reached down, removing the woman's hand from between her legs. She stood and slipped around the corner of the desk, grabbing up her shirt and slipping it quickly back on. She held the halves tight around her and stopped, tugging her skirt back down into place and staring out of the window.

"It's been a very long time since I've been alive." She turned her face a fraction, just the point of her noble nose showing past the sweep of her hair. "Perhaps you should go, Major."

Hawk's jaw dropped and she stood, the sting of fingernail grooves in her back anchoring her in disbelief. Embarrassment surged through her, followed quickly by an anger so intense she nearly flipped the desk in her rage. It seeped through her, ate at her guts. She stared daggers into the back of the woman who stood, calmly dismissing her with her back turned after the moment they had just shared.

She was a fool to think it had meant anything at all. Gail had even subtly warned her that it would mean nothing, and yet still, ridiculously, she had allowed herself to be lost in the lie. She stooped and grabbed her jacket, rushing to the door before she lost the tight control of her burning fury.

She reached for the doorknob, and a quiet, dead sort of voice spoke behind her. "Thank you."

Her humiliation was complete. She stared at the grain of the wood inches from her nose as though the words thundering too loudly in her brain might be etched in the mahogany. A thousand different responses to such a cruel comment pounded in time with her pulse. She gripped the jacket in her hand and felt a soft fabric trapped there. She must have picked up Gail's discarded panties as well in her rush to escape. She counted three breaths and still found no words to give voice to the emotion coursing through her.

She turned the knob and bolted through the door without a word, slamming it behind her with a most satisfying bang. She pretended not to hear the thud of Gail's body hitting the floor behind her or the wails of her sobs as she pounded down the hall.

CHAPTER TWENTY-TWO

Hawk's feet carried her through the compound without any input from her mind. She moved like a zombie, lucky not to bounce off the walls as she paced. The anger leaked out of her, leaving her empty and confused. She didn't notice the lights dim slightly or the temperature drop a degree. She saluted as she passed her men, more to make them drop their own arms than anything else. The smell of cigarette smoke clung to her and the taste of scotch and skin lingered on her tongue. Her senses, it seemed, would not allow her to forget the encounter.

She came to a stop and blinked, staring at tall plastic letters on the wall announcing the Clinic. The sounds echoing in her head changed from Gail's screams to Williams' screams. Maybe they'd been there all along. That must have been what brought her here.

If she had such a thing as a friend among her men, Williams would certainly qualify. She had shared innumerable beers with him, laughing at Forest's pathetic attempts to pick up women. Less than a week before they left Earth she had carried William's son on her shoulders at the North Carolina State Fair while he chased his daughter away from the pigpen and his wife, in her third trimester, tried not to succumb to the stifling heat.

Hawk realized that she needed to talk to someone, and he was the one. When she had stopped by on her way to Gail's office he had still been unconscious. Maybe it would be enough to sit quietly next to him and gather her thoughts.

She pushed open the door and immediately wished she hadn't. Williams was awake and sitting up in his bed. He looked a little the worse for wear. His left arm was heavily bandaged and anchored in a sling. Purpling bruises bloomed across his bare chest. Still, he was smiling and laughing. Laughing because Forest was there, his eyebrows waggling in that way that made even the most innocent situation indecent. If Hawk were to list those she would want to confide in after an intense but unexpected alcohol-fueled hook-up with a near stranger, Forest would literally be the last person on that list. She suddenly wished she had showered and changed before coming here.

"Major!" Williams finally spotted her and she forced a smile as she walked to the bed. "Everyone's coming out of the woodwork to hang out with me. I should get shot more often."

Forest punched him in his good shoulder hard enough to make him wince. "I'm surprised you don't get shot more often, Steve-o. Hate to break it to you, man, but you're a pretty lousy soldier. Almost Marine-level bad."

"Whoa, dude." He put on a brave face, but there was an audible wheeze when he laughed. "That's a low blow."

"True. You'd have to get shot in the head to be as dumb as a Marine."

The men laughed at the lame joke and the old rivalry, but Hawk was still distracted with her own thoughts and her own laugh was late and forced. Williams looked at her with a wrinkle in his brow, and Forest, normally so obtuse, picked up on the mood.

He stood and held out his hand to Williams, who shook it. "Glad you didn't get yourself killed, Steve." He moved toward the door with a respectful nod at Hawk and shouted over his shoulder, "I'd gladly fill in with that wife of yours, but I'm not daddy material."

Silence stretched between them long enough for Williams to shift on his bed. "That guy'll never grow up." He looked searchingly at Hawk, who couldn't think of a single thing to say. "What's up, Charlie?"

Hawk had always been commissioned, so the habit of officers calling each other by their first names was nothing unusual for her. Williams, however, had started his career as an enlisted man and won a Green to Gold scholarship. He worked hard, earned his degree, and was commissioned late in his career. The idea of addressing a fellow officer by their first name was foreign to him, and he rarely did. It was a dead giveaway she'd been found out. Her normally composed exterior must have slipped farther than she'd imagined.

"Just coming to check on you, Steve. Happy to see you aren't gonna die on me. If I had to deal with Forest alone I'd probably look forward to suffocating and freezing to death."

Williams looked down at his olive-drab socks and said quietly, "I'm sorry I couldn't secure the objective for you, Major."

Guilt flooded through her, the bitterness of it monumental, blocking out everything else. "That's not your fault, Steve. We were betrayed. You all did a hell of a job getting out of there in one piece."

"Not all of us."

He flexed his bandaged arm, but she knew he wasn't thinking about himself. There were three black bags in a freezer many floors below them and three empty pairs of boots outside tents back in The Docks. She would have three letters to write when they got back home. If they got back home.

"That's not your fault, Steve."

He looked up at her and his eyes were clear. "It isn't yours either, Charlie." He studied her face for a moment and continued, "But you know that. So I'll ask again, what's wrong?"

She leaned forward and breathed out low and slow, pressing the pad of her thumb to the bridge of her nose. "Gail."

"What about her?"

"I…" She couldn't get the words out so she changed tack. "She thinks we're all going to die. She's given up. Maybe her mood got to me."

She stared at the floor, but she heard the sound of his hand rasping over his stubbled chin. "You sure that's the only way she got to you?"

To her surprise, she didn't blush when she sat back and crossed her arms. "Don't know what you mean, Steve."

"Come on, Charlie. I've known you a long time. That woman's got your head spun." She looked away and he laughed, the wheeze stronger this time. "I knew it. You've got it bad, boss. I'll admit, she's hot, but I didn't take you for the type to go for someone so…"

"Cold? Calculating? Manipulative? Heartless?"

"I wouldn't say heartless or cold. Maybe you haven't noticed since you don't get to see her with her folks, but she is caring to the point of coddling with most of them. There's this one girl. I think she's new up here or something, and she's crying all the time. Ms. Moore sits with her for hours, talking to her, calming her down. Benton and his team are guarding the housing block with those idiots from the security force, and he said she's barely spent an hour in there since we landed. She'll go up and change and come right back down."

Hawk's brain wasn't really keeping up with his speech. She swallowed hard and saw the exhausted slump of Gail's shoulders. The bags under her eyes.

"To be honest, she reminds me a lot of you."

"Of me?"

He sat forward, leaning toward her as best he could with his immobilized arm. "Every man and woman here knows that you would gladly lay down your life for any one of us. I'd be willing to bet her people feel the same way. Even that girl you nearly put a bullet in. Forest said she's been crying since you left. Weeping about 'letting her down' and 'betraying the boss'. Seems like it never occurred to her that helping that madman might get people hurt."

"Yeah, well, it doesn't matter, Steve. It just wouldn't…"

"Cut the bullshit, Charlie." She snapped her head up and he looked apologetic for a split second. "Stop playing the martyr and go ask her out."

"I beg your pardon, Captain?"

"Don't get indignant on me. God knows you've been carrying around your imaginary cross for too damn long." She opened her mouth to shout at him, but he fired back before she could start, "You could've been married a dozen times over, but you won't let anyone get close to you. You pretend like it's because you dedicate yourself to the Army, but really you're just scared. Scared to let anyone get close and now you're giving her shit for doing the same thing?"

"You better watch..."

"No." He gritted his teeth and spat his words out. "You've had to fight against impossible odds to get where you are, I'm not denying that. But you could have done with someone who loved you. You chose to do it alone. Now you're just old and bitter and it doesn't look good on you, ma'am."

She was on her feet, her finger inches from his face. "You keep waggin' your jaw and I'll break it for you!" He started laughing and she couldn't help but feel a little ridiculous. "And I'm not old, you little shit."

"Nice to finally see you riled up." He pressed his free hand to his bruised ribs and winced, letting her calm down and drop back into her chair. "Okay, you aren't old, but you're sure as shit out of practice. Go ask her out."

"Oh, right. I'll invite her to dinner at the little French restaurant down the street. We can schedule it for right after we all turn into ice-cube corpses."

He waved his hand dismissively. "You'll figure out a way to get us out of this. Besides, no one goes to dinner for first dates any more. Too intimate. Coffee for the first date."

"Okay, maybe I am a little out of practice."

"A little? I'm asking this as a friend. Have you been on a date during a year that didn't start with nineteen?"

"Fuck you."

"I didn't think so."

Hawk rubbed a hand through her hair. "Anyway, we're a little beyond a first date."

"Yeah, I know." He pointed to the cargo pocket just above her right knee. "I didn't think those were your style."

A loop of red lace stuck out from the pocket, the elastic band wrapped around the button at the back of the pocket. She felt the heat on her face as she fought to free the panties and shove them out of sight. When she shrugged into her jacket after leaving Gail's office she had found them in her hand and, not knowing what to do with them, shoved them into the pocket without looking.

"Oh, fuck. I'm never going to live this down, am I?"

"When Forest saw them? No chance at all. Although, I think that bite mark on your neck will have him talking more." His smile was so genuine, she couldn't help but join in. "You ask me, it's about time you got laid."

She buried her head in her hands, her heart thumping painfully against her ribs. "She's… It's not like that." She gripped angry fistfuls of her own hair. "What's she done to me, Steve?"

"Whoa, are you in love with her?"

His skepticism was obvious, but something about what he said actually felt right to her. She only examined the thought for a moment before dismissing it. "No. I barely know her."

"I didn't ask if you know her, I asked if you love her."

"No. I can't. I just… I don't know. We left it in a bad place."

"Then go fix it."

"I can't. Time is running out here, Steve. There are more important things."

"Stop." His face was stern again. "I have a wife back at Bragg who makes my head spin even after all these years. I made an oath to my country, but God knows I'm not a robot. Neither are you. General Harris would kick your ass if he knew you'd consider ignoring this. We need time to rest and recover. We need time to plan. Go find that girl, you idiot."

CHAPTER TWENTY-THREE

Glass pressed against Gail's cheek like a sheet of ice. Her tears had stopped some time ago, but she still felt their trails, dry and stretching the skin of her face. Her eyes were puffy and she didn't have the strength to open them. Her body was stiff and sore from sitting on the hard floor for too long. It ached in a myriad of places, but nowhere so much as in her chest, where her lungs were small and tight and could not fill with air.

Gail let herself slip into thoughtlessness. She swam in emptiness for a long time, her normally active mind set free to wander without course.

Once, when Gail was a teenager and still had the spark of adventure passed down through her grandmother's spirit, she had snuck off late at night. The reservation had an old quarry, an unnatural hole cut deep into a mesa. It had been abandoned and filled with water to provide a swimming hole for the tribe. When Gail snuck out of her house and down to the quarry, she'd been a teenager with raging hormones. She'd found her first girlfriend there waiting for her on the shore and they made love under the new moon, their voices bouncing off stone and water.

When her girlfriend fell asleep, Gail slipped naked into the cold water and floated out to the very center. She lay on her back, her arms spread wide and her body bobbing on the surface like an offering to the stars. She floated there, staring at the dark sky until she could see the shadowy silhouette of the moon and felt her eyelids grow heavy.

Her fascination with death and her teenage sense of invincibility warred within her, enticing her to let her eyes close, let her body slip under the black water. The thought had frightened her and her girlfriend called out to her to come in at the same moment. She swam hard for the shore, trying to leave the thought out there in the center of the lake, far away from her.

Gail had chosen to swim that night. But tonight she would let herself fall asleep and slip beneath the surface. Her fear was gone now, pressed into the willing flesh of another. She was alone in the night and she let herself see that moonless sky from her youth. Someone called her name and there was a sound like a hand striking wood, but she would ignore her girlfriend this time. That had been their last night together anyway. She'd been dumped a week later and Gail wondered if it had been the chill of seeing her in the center of the lake that night that had severed their tenuous connection. It wouldn't have mattered if she'd stayed in the lake then and it wouldn't matter now.

Settling back into the recollection of the quarry, Gail felt colder than she had that night as a teenager. A distant part of her mind told her it was because the batteries were running low. The station was slowly shutting itself down to preserve power. Soon the whole of Moon Base would do what she was doing now, slip beneath the surface of the lake, never to return. The thought was not borne of fear but of realism. She acknowledged the thought. Examined it and sent it floating away from her. There was nothing to be done about it now.

Gail's ears were underwater now, and strange sounds filled them from far away. Footsteps and a voice, low but insistent, near her. She wondered for a moment if her girlfriend had decided to dive in and join her. Someone was close by. Gail could feel someone else in the room.

She didn't truly feel the cold of her skin until Hawk touched her cheek. Her fingers were so warm against Gail's face that they burned. She flinched away on instinct and pressed back in on need. Cold. She was so cold. She tried to look around her but she saw only shapes moving underwater, indistinct blurs. She tried to speak, but her lips would not move and all she could manage was a whimper that sounded, even to her own ears, like a thing without life.

* * *

When Hawk reentered the office she thought it was empty. It was so dark, darker than the outer office or the halls. The glow from the wall of windows, the bleed from the other domes, provided most of the light. The desk was as she had left it. The stale, overflowing ashtray and the pair of empty glasses at the center next to the half full bottle of scotch. Gail's bra dangled precariously from the edge, and Hawk had a vivid memory of the taste of her skin. Like pine needles, vanilla, and sweat. A shiver ran through her body and she forced herself to move on from the sight.

No one had answered when Hawk knocked and called Gail's name. Still, she sensed that Gail was still here. There was a soft sound from the other side of the desk. Like the whimper of a dying animal. She moved forward and finally saw Gail. She was in the same spot against the window where she had stood when she sent Hawk away, but she was slumped on the floor, legs curled beneath her, upper body leaning against the thick glass of the window. Her hair was a mess, the long, stick-straight dark strands sticking out at odd angles, knotted and mussed. The point of her chin and one smooth cheek was visible, and the skin was ghostly pale. Her mouth hung slightly open and her arms were limp. Had it not been for the sound she had made, Hawk would fear she was dead.

She knelt close enough to touch, but Gail made no move to acknowledge her presence. She reached out a trembling hand and slid the hair back from her face. Her fingertip brushed against Gail's cheek, and the skin was as cold as it looked. She felt the woman trembling, the silk shirt rustling like leaves in a wind. When she tucked the lock of hair behind Gail's ear, she looked up with vacant eyes. They landed on Hawk's features, but did not seem to take them in at all. She raised her hand and trailed her fingers along the square line of Hawk's jaw and a single tear fell from the corner of her eye, tracing a path over her high cheekbones and disappearing behind her ear.

Hawk slipped an arm under Gail's knees and the other below her outstretched arm. She stood, picking up the slight woman and cradling her limp body against her chest. Gail did not as much as gasp at the show of strength. She sat quietly, allowing herself to be carried from the room. By the time Hawk made it to the stairwell, Gail's head had slumped against her shoulder.

As the most senior corporate official on Moon Base, Gail's apartment was the most opulent. It occupied nearly half of the highest floor of living quarters, just two floors down from her office. Hawk's back ached with the strain of carrying her down stairs and through endless corridors, but not nearly as much as it should have. The lowered gravity of the station certainly had benefited her, but she was happy to see the large plastic numbers on the wall next to her door. It took a great deal of maneuvering to hold Gail's limp form and also unclip the ID badge from her waistband. Fortunately, she only had to hold it to the electronic sensor by the door and the lock clicked open.

Low lighting flicked on automatically, and she was able to make her way down a short hall to the bedroom. She was as gentle as possible when she set Gail on the edge of the bed. To her surprise, the woman stayed upright. Her head lolled and she slumped visibly, but she stayed in a sitting position. Looking over her shoulders to scan the room, she found an open door on the far side with a tile floor stretching beneath it.

"Don't move." She stood, her knees popping. "I'll be right back."

The shower was in the far corner of the room. A curving tiled wall that ended several feet from the ceiling defined the space. It was fortunate that she wouldn't have to contend with either a tub or a door, and she spun the handle farther to the hot water side than she normally would have. Steam filled the room.

Gail still sat impassively, her head lolling forward and her hair shielding her face from view. A pang of sympathy stabbed Hawk's chest, and she moved slowly to the woman's side. Gail looked up, but her eyes were still vague. Hawk knelt in front of her and reached for her foot, cradling the ankle as she slipped off first one shoe, then the other. She slipped her thumbs under the top of her thigh highs and peeled them off.

The confusion on Gail's face increased, and Hawk gave her what she hoped came across as a reassuring smile. She supported her as she helped her to her feet and held her in place with a strong arm around her waist as she unzipped the skirt and let it fall to the ground. Easing her back to sit on the bed again was more a graceful fall, and her body shivered as Hawk slid the shirt off her shoulders.

The detachment with which Gail sat, naked and shivering, on the edge of the bed made Hawk less careful about removing her own clothes. The sound of Velcro tearing set her teeth, but she quickly managed to strip down to just her T-shirt and boxer briefs. Something inside her rebelled at the way her uniform lay crumpled on the floor, the American flag patch just visible in the mess, but she forced her mind back to the woman in front of her. Her hands were gentle as she slipped her arms back around Gail and lifted her to rest against her chest again. Gail was limp and heavy in her arms, but a small sigh escaped her when Hawk held her close.

She flinched when the warm jets of water hit her chilled skin, and she burrowed farther into the shelter of Hawk's embrace. The water flooded over her, relaxing and warming her body.

"I'm going to put you down on your feet. Can you stand on your own?"

When she nodded against Hawk's wet shoulder, the soldier lowered her and set her on her feet so gently that half her weight was on them before she felt the floor. She leaned back against the slick tile and closed her eyes. She stood far enough away from the shower's spray that it hit just at mid-thigh, but close enough so that she was still wrapped in the mist and steam. Her knees wobbled unsteadily but held. Hawk moved around the shower, inspecting bottles, but always keeping one eye on Gail. Something told her that, if she left now, Gail would simply slide to a ball on the floor and let the world speed by above her.

The heady scent of vanilla filled the shower as Hawk rubbed soap into a washcloth. She touched the soft cloth to Gail's arm as gently as she could, but still she jumped. Gail's eyes flew open and darted around the room like a feral cat before settling on her. Hawk held the sudsy washcloth still, waiting for Gail to relax. She let out her breath in short puffs and Hawk turned her eyes back to the cloth, rubbing it gently across her skin, up to her slumped shoulder. She lifted Gail's hand and held it up so she could wash her. She shifted, but kept her body at a respectful distance. Suds trailed across Gail's chest, and the cloth washed the length of her neck and then back up to her hairline. After the other arm, Hawk moved the cloth to her chest, clinically washing her breasts before moving to her abdomen. Hawk forced herself to swallow both her pity and her lust.

"Turn."

She kept her voice smooth and compelling and, to her surprise, Gail turned to face the tile wall without hesitation. Hawk closed her eyes and lost herself in the feel of the soft body beneath her hands. There was nothing sexual about her movements, but they were so achingly intimate that something inside her chest swelled pleasantly and her eyes stung and prickled. Gail tried to lean back into the body she could sense behind her, but Hawk darted away.

She didn't want the warmth growing inside her to ruin this moment. To turn it from the comfort Gail needed to the desire Hawk felt. There was time for that another day. A day when Gail was herself.

Lowering herself to her knees, she washed Gail's legs. She had to keep her focus narrow, but she felt the change in Gail's breathing. Gail reached a hand out to the wall to steady herself, and Hawk was on her feet in an instant, a supporting hand on her waist.

"Are you okay?"

"Yes…" She choked on the word. "No."

Hawk's hand moved around her waist and Gail melted back into her. The water pounded against their feet and splashed up to tickle Hawk's calves. She could feel Gail's breathing come heavily and fast and suddenly she needed the woman more than she had ever needed anything in her life. More than she needed air. Even while she was telling herself to quash that need, Gail groped for Hawk's other hand and wrapped it around herself, cradling the clenched fist in her own hand and pressing it hard into the soft skin of the valley between her breasts. She turned her head, reaching up with her free hand to pull Hawk down into a kiss.

Hawk's lips moved of their own accord, matching Gail's. A hand slid to the back of Hawk's head gripping hard at the wet strands of hair plastered to her skull. She yearned to feel Gail's fingers run through that hair again, to grip fistfuls of it. Gail parted her lips, begging for her to deepen the kiss, but instead she pulled back.

"That's not what this is about. I wasn't trying to get you…"

"I know." Gail cut her off and rushed to get her own words out. "I know, but I want you. Please?"

Hawk hadn't realized how tense she was until the plea softened her. The stress flooded out of her body and she released Gail, spinning her back around and pinning her to the wall with the weight of her body. She pulled Gail to her and pushed against her at the same time, the wall supporting them both in the fire of their need. Hawk's kisses were gentle but insistent and she felt Gail's body respond to them. She had no idea how much time had passed since they had last touched, but it could not have been more than an hour. Still, the ache inside her was painfully strong, as though their time together had multiplied rather than satisfied her need. Gail reached for the band of Hawk's underwear with hands made shaky with impatience.

Hawk laid a hand on hers to stop her. "No. Let me take care of you. If we're going to die, I want you to die feeling something."

She didn't want to hear if Gail would respond. Tears sparkled unshed but threatening in Gail's eyes and Hawk didn't trust herself to watch them fall. Actions had always served her better than words anyway. Her lips trailed down Gail's jaw and across her throat. Hawk's lips trailed down Gail's chest, pausing to linger at her breasts to elicit a groan from her. Gail gripped Hawk's shoulders so hard her knuckles went white. Hawk's mouth was moving on and she dropped wet, openmouthed kisses on the points of Gail's hipbones despite the soap bubbles still clinging to them.

Hawk's knees made a hollow splash as they hit the floor, and she found suddenly that she wasn't ready. She wanted to feel, but she was afraid of being swept away. It had been so long since anyone had touched her, either her body or her heart, and she had become uncomfortably sensitive to the experience. Giving Gail this piece of her, this moment of light in a day so dark, became harder than anything else she had ever done. It felt raw. Exposed, though she was the one still clothed. In the moment she found that, despite her intention to provide solace to Gail, she took as much for herself. Perhaps that had always been part of her intention.

Hawk wavered for a heartbeat, but she knew what she would do. She knew what she wanted and it was right in front of her. The heat of her mouth enveloped Gail, cradling her rather than possessing her. When she moved her lips and her tongue it was delicate and honey-sweet. She picked up her pace and moved with a determination that had Gail clawing at the wall for some sort of purchase. When Gail cried out, Hawk's hands went to her hips, holding her in place as her pleasure built. Her release came shuddering and hard, catching them both by surprise. She screamed to the ceiling and still Hawk surged forward, unrelenting, wringing burst after burst of pleasure from her.

It all became too much. Hawk's heart, pounding at a different rhythm than she had ever known, skipped until she thought she might crumble to the tile floor, but Gail crumpled first. Her legs would not support her any longer. She started to slip, but Hawk's hands were there to catch her. She guided Gail down with strong hands. Then she shifted her own body and they were sitting in each other's arms, under the rapidly cooling spray of the shower.

Hawk stared at Gail's face. She wanted to memorize it. Brand this image onto her brain so that, when the final moment came, however it came, this would be what she saw. The sweep of her hair, droplets of water beading and dripping from the stray lock that refused to stay tucked behind her ear. The set of her jaw and the slightest downturn of her lips. She wore sadness well. The tragic stillness of her features carried unmatched dignity. But mostly her eyes. Hawk wanted to remember her eyes. Those golden-brown circles that promised her nothing and yet somehow offered endless possibilities.

Exhaustion came upon her again and Gail's eyes slipped closed. Hawk watched with a growing weight in her own eyelids, but a lifetime of disciplined insomnia worked in her favor now. Hawk watched Gail's chest rise and fall. Watched the lines of pain and worry smooth out. Most people looked younger when they slept, but not this woman. She was an ageless creature to start with and the loosening of her earthly cares did not change that.

Hawk sat on the floor of the shower, holding Gail in her arms as a yellow light flickered to red by the showerhead and the water abruptly cut off.

CHAPTER TWENTY-FOUR

Sound filled Gail's world. Deafening noise all mixed together. Ululating voices of singers praying at the Sun Dance. Kokopelli's flute whistling in her ears. Pounding of moccasin-wrapped feet on beaten earth. The slow, steady beat of drums in unison. They swirled around her in a rising cacophony. What had always been comforting was suddenly terrifying and her heart screamed for the sound to stop.

As though in answer to her command, it did. Not just the singing or the music or the swishing of rough fabric and treated animal hides. Everything. All sound winked out in the blink of an eye. The silence pressed at her ears like water leaking through her eardrums. At first it was frightening, then it was soothing to feel the weight of that silence.

She was weightless. Floating. Her body light and free as it had not been in longer than she could remember. Maybe lighter than it had ever been. Her eyes saw nothing. Only the blackness of a void. Darkness so absolute it held her in place. Held her in an icy grip. It was otherworldly. Impossible. It was too dark to see the universe. She turned her head and opened her eyes as wide as they could go, but no light found its way in. The darkness spread through her like a poison thick as tar.

She reached down and touched her own body to be sure it was there, and, in doing so, she gave it weight. Too much weight. She was falling, the lack of gravity a trick of her mind that was plummeting through the empty oblivion toward who knew what.

She wanted to scream, but she needed breath to force out the terror in her chest. She opened her mouth to breathe, discovering as she did so that there was no air around her. No oxygen. Only ice-cold nothingness wrapped in a blanket of blackest night. She was suffocating. She was falling and she was blind and she couldn't breathe. The collective force of all of these fears gave her voice and the scream ripped from her.

She woke up sweating, her body shaking with the force of her nightmare, and her scream echoing off the walls. It was dark, but not absolutely. Low light glowed from unseen sources at strange angles. She could make out the bedroom around her, feel the sheets wrapped around her writhing legs. Her naked body thrashed, sending pillows and sheets flying. Then an arm like steel wrapped around her and pinned her arms to her side. The arm drew her in, and she stopped kicking her legs. She was pulled tight against a muscular torso and a pair of small, firm breasts. Hawk's voice was in her ear, sleepily murmuring calming words.

She tried to relax, tried to tell herself it was just a dream, but the air felt thin, insubstantial. She gulped at it and only felt more panicked. Worse still, the feeling of falling would not leave her. She felt as though she would fall away from this moment and be back in that dark vortex. She would float away from here and be lost forever. Lost and no one left to search for her. She sobbed again and Hawk's arm tightened over her chest. The muscles bunched and she ran her palm along the woman's bicep, feeling the dips and bulges of defined strength. She focused on that feeling. If Hawk held her she would stay here, in this moment. She would be safe.

"Hawk?"

"Shh…it's okay. It was only a dream. Only a dream. You're okay."

"Please…"

"It's okay. I'm here. What do you need?"

Gail scrabbled at Hawk's well-built arm. She gulped and held tight to Hawk's skin, trying to wring from its solid warmth the answer to her question. Trying desperately to make her panic-soaked brain come up with knowledge of what she needed. She pulled Hawk closer, knowing only that she felt better when their skin touched.

Hawk slipped a leg over Gail. Something inside Gail loosened a fraction.

"Charlie…"

She pulled at Hawk's side, trying to move beneath her. Maybe it was how abruptly Hawk had awoken, but she wasn't moving as quickly as she normally did. Fortunately, since her brain didn't appear to be responding, she let Gail lead her actions. Shifting her body, Gail wedged herself between Hawk and the mattress until she finally seemed to understand. She rolled and then Gail could breathe fully again. The weight of Hawk's nearly limp body pressed down on her, anchoring her to the moment by pinning her to the bed. She wrapped arms and legs around Hawk's body and sighed with an almost childlike contentment.

"Better?" Hawk's groggy voice echoed in the darkness.

She nodded, her chin tapping against Hawk's broad shoulder. With the solid form of this woman on top of her, she could finally breathe, finally be safe. She ran her fingers over Hawk's back, feeling the sharp peaks of her vertebrae. Hawk shuddered above her as her fingers trailed down to the corded muscle of her lower back.

Her hands danced across Hawk's skin and she felt in that moment the bliss she had been without for far too long. Not the giving or receiving of pleasure but the intimacy. The sensuality of another's body pressed against hers. Still, in the dark and stillness of this night she knew that it was not merely intimacy, but this particular intimacy that stilled her racing heart and quieted the panic that filled her. Intimacy with this person in this moment.

Gail refocused on her breathing. Her body was slow to still, but eventually she started to slip back into sleep. She knew it would be a calm, restful interlude. As her breathing slowed, Hawk shifted her weight, preparing to slide back onto the bed.

"No. Stay." Gail gripped tight at her side with both hands. "Please? I need you to hold me down."

There was questioning in Hawk's eyes, but no judgment. She smiled and nodded, settling back above her and giving Gail most of her weight. The solidity of her was enough. She was almost asleep again, Hawk's weight anchoring her in place, when the thought ran through her mind that the last fear of the nightmare was gone. All that was left was this, and she drifted back to sleep with something dangerously close to a grin on her face.

CHAPTER TWENTY-FIVE

Pillows surrounded Gail when she woke. Her face was buried deep in the foamy mass of one, the weight of another on her scalp, and a third gripped so tightly between her arms and legs that her fingers ached from clenching. She fought to separate herself from them, but a tangle of sheet, blanket and comforter worked against her. Her coordination was not its best, and the ache of a hangover pounding in her temple and the acrid taste of stale tobacco smoke thick on her tongue were weighing her down. It brought the memories of the previous night home to her. Not only what had transpired in her office, but rich, heady flashes of the shower and then flinging off the sheets to be covered by something else in the middle of the night. She stopped struggling and let the smile spread across her face.

She carefully pushed the pillow off her head and onto the floor. She listened for sounds in the room and was disappointed to be met by absolute silence. She reached out. Her hands slid across the impossible softness of the Egyptian cotton sheets and met nothing but wrinkles. She turned her face toward the opposite side of the bed. It was empty. She raised her head to look into the bathroom. Nothing but a disheveled mess of towels on the tiled floor. She sat up a little too quickly and gripped her head. When the wave of nausea passed she looked around. Her garments were spread haphazardly around the plush carpet, but there was no sign of olive-drab or pixelated camouflage. Gail let out a long breath and let her body flop back on the mattress.

She stared at the ceiling, willing her foggy mind to replay the night's events, sadness flooding through her. The stolen cigarettes. Cracking the seal on the bottle of scotch. Hawk arriving. Sharing more of her story than she had in years. Dragging the woman to her. Then her vulnerability. Her cruel words. The sadness coming back as a tsunami. She'd been so tired. The fear and the scotch and the intensity of the encounter drained her more than she could stand.

That part was real. Then there were strong arms lifting her and carrying her here. The shower. The things that were said. Followed by troubled sleep. A calming interruption and more sleep. Deeper than she'd allowed herself in days. Weeks really. Since she'd known trouble was brewing. Since the first whispers of threat to the people she was responsible for.

It had been a dream. It had to have been. It was too perfect. Too blissful. The words had been exactly right. The touch so soft. Hawk couldn't have known, couldn't have read her mind like that. Of course not. She hadn't been here. She had been a dream. A desire born of guilt and exhaustion and desperate need. But it had been a delusion, and it was done now. She was alone. Still, it had felt so real. She reached out and ran her hand over the empty space beside her, but it was cold. No one had slept beside her last night. She'd conjured that comfort out of thin air. It was a spirit that danced beside her when she needed it most but evaporated while she slept.

She stood on stiff legs and moved toward the bathroom, ignoring the pile of clothes and the larger pile of towels. Her hair was a tangled mess that took a long time to tame. She brushed her teeth twice, cursing herself for giving in to the temptation to smoke. Examining her face in the mirror, she found that the hollowness of her cheeks was not as prominent and the bags that had settled under her eyes were a little less puffy than they had been the day before. Maybe the Major had not held her while she slept, but she had, at the very least, allowed her the first good night's sleep she'd had in a long time. With a last, uncharacteristically wistful sigh she wrapped her robe around herself.

As she made her way into the open living space, the first thing that struck her was the smell of fresh brewed coffee. The second thing, and it brought her to a dead stop, was the person seated in her dining nook. Hawk sat on one side of the little bistro table, head bent over a laptop, scribbling notes on a legal pad beside her. Her jaw was set and she stared at the screen. She was in full uniform, creases crisp and razor straight. Her boots were planted firmly on the floor, the back of her heels touching the legs of her chair and her shoulders were thrown back. Gail reached out and gripped the doorframe.

Hawk did not look up, but, when she finished writing, she picked up a steaming cup of coffee, depositing it in front of the other chair. She continued typing as though nothing had happened. Gail's stomach churned uncomfortably as she realized that last night had not been a dream or a drunken hallucination after all. After a few silent moments, Hawk lifted a foot under the table and pushed at the empty chair. It slid noisily out from under the table leaf a few inches and Hawk brought her boot back down, her typing never wavering.

Gail couldn't ignore the invitation and fought to keep her gait steady as she walked over to the chair. She looked away to hide her smile as she sat down and picked up the mug, cupping it in her hands to draw out warmth from the ceramic. The coffee was strong and black, and she tried to remember if she had ever told Hawk that she never used cream or sugar. The thought slipped from her mind as she traced the long column of the woman's neck with her eyes. She saw the bruise and imprint of teeth at the base and a blush spread from her cheeks down her neck.

Hawk set down the pen abruptly and Gail lowered her eyes back to her coffee, not sure if she was ready to say anything yet. She felt rather than saw the major stand and move to the counter, happy for a few moments to allow her brain to catch up with the astonishing events. Then the warmth of Hawk's body was at her side. A plate appeared in front of her, still warm from the oven, piled high with eggs and bacon and buttery toast. Her stomach growled unexpectedly at the sight and she tried to remember the last time she'd eaten. Then Hawk put down a tall glass of orange juice and a pair of aspirin.

Hawk's hand was still cool from the glass as it wrapped around Gail's cheek, gently compelling her to look up. Their eyes locked for the first time this morning, and Gail saw the twinkle of a smile. Hawk lowered her lips and caught hers in a kiss. She ended it far too quickly for Gail's liking, pulling away with her mouth still firmly closed and retreating to her own seat. Gail's head spun, but her mouth curved up and her heart was racing.

"What's…" Gail looked around, feeling like she'd just stepped through the looking glass. "What's this?"

"Breakfast."

"Charlie!" Annoyance swelled in her and she glared hard at Hawk, who just smiled back. "Talk to me."

Hawk laid down her pen and closed her laptop. Lacing her fingers together in front of her, she rested her chin on them, squinting across the table. "You had quite a night." Gail felt herself blush again, but there was not a hint of self-consciousness in the soldier's eyes. "And you are in for a long day. So eat your eggs and drink your juice. I need you sharp. Okay?"

Gail picked up her fork as her stomach growled again. It wasn't long before she was attacking the food eagerly and Hawk's eyes were back on her notes. After the first pangs of her hunger were satisfied, she paused and asked hesitantly, "When you say that I'm in for a long day…"

"Keep it in your pants, woman, that's not what I meant." She shot Gail a wink and another lopsided grin that made her bite her bottom lip. "There will be plenty of time for that later."

The eggs turned to concrete in her mouth and she could barely swallow. "I'm not so sure about that."

"I am." The cold determination in her stare was almost enough to convince Gail that she meant it. "You need your strength because today is the day we get out of here. Today we end all of this."

"How?"

Hawk reopened her laptop. "Finish your breakfast. Then get dressed. Debrief is in thirty minutes."

Gail rolled her eyes at the bossiness in her tone but set to work on her breakfast again.

"I saw that."

Gail chewed, trying not to let the happy bubble in her chest grow. She had too much experience with the pain that comes after the bubble bursts to let herself succumb to it now. Still, her eyes were drawn to the woman whose words last night came flooding back. She wondered how bad it would be if, this one time, she did let herself feel something.

Hawk's eyes flicked up, catching her stare, and then went to her motionless fork. "Eat."

"I…um…" She flew back into motion, grabbing a piece of toast and fiddling with the crust. "I'm sorry about your neck. I have some concealer if you want."

"It's fine. The damage has been done, I'm afraid." She rubbed at the base of her neck. "Forest already saw it, so I'm sure the whole company knows by now."

"Sorry."

Hawk sat back and crossed her arms over her chest. "Don't worry, I'm sure I can find an appropriate punishment for you when this is all over."

"I look forward to it," Gail smirked as she took the last piece of toast into the bedroom.

CHAPTER TWENTY-SIX

Hawk chose to hold the war council in one of the corporate conference rooms instead of down in The Docks. For this particular meeting she required several more civilians besides Gail, and she thought they might feel more at ease meeting up here instead of in a noisy, crowded tent while her men converted the hangar into a staging area. It was the same conference room where she had called to Earth and talked to Harris, and she couldn't help but wonder if that was the last contact she'd ever get to have with her friend and CO.

She and Gail arrived late, but not remarkably so. They walked in together and Hawk braced herself for the whispers and winks. But, other than the standard salute, there was no visible reaction from any of her people. Perhaps Forest had finally learned to keep his mouth shut.

They separated as soon as they entered the room, Hawk moving off to the knot of officers and Gail walking up to the three civilians who were standing off to the side, looking intimidated and out of place. They gave a collective double take when they saw her, which they quickly turned into welcoming smiles. Hawk couldn't blame them. She may have known Gail far shorter a time than her employees, but the outfit she had appeared in after her shower this morning had been a shock.

Her hair was pulled back into a tight ponytail that rode high on her head and her makeup was flattering but minimal. She wore a pair of black compression running pants with a pink stripe down the side and worn gray running shoes. Her jacket was also designed for running, made of thick, breathable fabric and a standing collar. Hawk could see the hint of a matching compression shirt beneath with a low scooped collar.

Something of her shock must have shown on her face, because Gail had pulled at the hem of her jacket and asked, "What?"

"Nothing."

She'd spoken too quickly and Gail looked even more uncomfortable. "I can't exactly wear a power suit to a council of war, can I? And I don't have a lot of casual clothes. My gym gear seemed appropriate."

"It is. Really, it's just…" Hawk had let her eyes run the length of Gail's slim legs and lingered on the tight hold the pants had on her thighs and butt. "I'm just going to have to watch Captain Forest's eyes, that's all."

"I considered asking you for a uniform, but I thought that might make people talk."

Her mind painted a very detailed image of Gail dressed in her uniform, or at least one or two pieces of it. She stood abruptly and headed for the door, willing the tantalizing image from her head as quickly as possible.

"You look great. Let's go."

She had definitely caught sight of a smirk on Gail's face as she passed through the door that Hawk held, and she almost certainly did not normally walk with that much of a sway to her hips.

Forest did not look. In fact, after he dropped his salute, he focused an undue amount of attention on the schematics lining the table. Hawk decided she needed to take the bull by the horns. "Been back to see Williams this morning? How does he look?"

"Not bad, ma'am." He looked up at her and the mischievous twinkle was still in his eye. He dropped his voice so that only the two of them could hear. "Been too busy to make it down to the Clinic this morning, Charlie?"

Hawk clasped her hands behind her back and flexed onto the balls of her feet. She pretended to be studying the floorplans. "Last night, too, Jerry. And if I so much as catch you looking at her ass I will make sure they never find your body."

"Calm down, boss. I wouldn't dream of it." She could see his smile out of the corner of her eye. "Nice work, Charlie. Seriously. She's hot. Not that I was looking or anything. So you gonna be a little less of a tight ass now that you got a piece of t…"

She stood up and turned to him, speaking in her normal voice again. "Not a chance in hell, Captain."

She heard him chuckle as she walked away to greet the civilians.

In consultation with her officers, Hawk had selected a trio of civilians to join the meeting today. She would've involved Gail in their selection, but the decision had to be made while Gail was still asleep. Personnel files were really all they'd had to go on, so this was her first chance to critique her choice.

The first good sign came in Gail's obvious warmth toward all of the attendees. There was none of the thinly veiled disgust she'd shown for Derek Drumm. She showed the most obvious kindness to an older man with thinning gray hair and a heavy stomach. He seemed the most relaxed of the group. Searching her memory for his name, Hawk finally settled on Randy Phelps. He was head of Information and Technology Services, the most likely person to help with locating the Caesar Terminal.

Next to him was a much younger and shorter man with a thick, bushy mustache and a stained denim shirt. Cordell Gates had the rich brown skin tone that seemed to glow with hues of orange and yellow in the right light. He was Head of Environmental Services, a blanket term that in this case covered janitorial services, but also maintenance of the facility at large, a much more demanding role here on the Moon than it would have been on Earth. He held an advanced degree in engineering, just like the woman standing beside him.

Hawk's knowledge of engineering was limited, but what she understood from their files, this woman, Stephanie Gilliard, was several notches above Gates on the corporate ladder. Her specialty was aerospace engineering, which gave her seniority and it was obvious from her manner. She held an air of the board room that was accentuated by her crisp khakis and horn-rimmed glasses. It was that air more than her position that now made Hawk doubt her usefulness here today. Still, if only one of her experts was less than helpful, she still had a decent chance.

Gail had spread her attention evenly among the group, only pausing her friendly chatter when Hawk approached.

Turning to the room at large, Hawk raised her voice. "Okay, gather in everyone. Clock's ticking."

The soldiers lined the table and stood at attention as was their habit, but, other than Gail, the civilians still looked nervous. They moved toward the table, but they watched their boss for guidance.

Gail spoke first, "Major, my colleagues tell me that they've been consulting with your men about a plan. Could you fill me in?"

"I think Captain Forest would be better suited to that role. Captain?"

"Yes, ma'am." He leaned over one of the floorplans laid out on the table. "Before the power went out, Mr. Drumm was able to provide us with access to some of the security features of Moon Base. Thermal scans of the prisoners' wing showed that most of them are staying pretty close to their cafeteria."

He indicated the cafeteria and the blocked corridor on his map.

"We know that the Caesar Protocol was put into effect just before the power was cut, and that means there is a single master computer terminal controlling everything somewhere over there and keeping us in danger. Mr. Phelps has indicated several computers that could be the Caesar terminal. There is no full-access terminal inside the cafeteria, so it has to be in another area of the wing."

Phelps spoke up, squinting at the map and pointing out several potential spots that had been circled. "It's probably in either the security substation here at the end of the hall leading to the ag dome or in the kitchen offices right outside the cafeteria. I can't imagine he would trudge all the way up to the security stations by the housing block entrance or across to the livestock dome entrance, for instance. It just wouldn't make sense to bypass those other two options."

Hawk answered the question in Gail's eyes, "We need to get to the Caesar Terminal before our batteries run out or we're all done. Once we get a team there we can open the doors and get everyone into a safe zone before we work on restoring the power over here. With the wing secured we can worry about trying to restore full function to the rest of the station and begin an evacuation plan."

Gail stared hard at the floorplan, saying, "Each of these potential sites is well within the boundaries of the area under the prisoners' control." She looked up, meeting Hawk's eye. "How do you propose to get there without fighting your way right through all of them?"

Hawk kept her face neutral as Forest answered, "That's exactly what we propose to do." She looked at him, her brow furrowed. "Fight our way right through them, I mean. At least that's what they think we're doing. Mr. Gates has provided us with some basic equipment we will need to cut our way through the barrier door that they locked down"

Gates cleared his throat, looking sheepishly at his superior. "Blow torches. Welding equipment. High-powered drills. All the stuff we use to do exterior repairs and work on the space planes, but I doubt they'll be able to bring down that big honkin' thing. It's meant to protect us from everything including loss of environment. It might take nothing less than a bomb to get through it."

"We've got that too if we need it." Hawk said, "But this is just a diversion. It isn't meant to be successful."

Something of the truth was dawning on Gail. "A diversion from what, exactly?"

Forest pointed to a series of chambers a dozen yards behind the cafeteria. "A small team will exit this wing of the compound and make their way around the dome to this airlock. They will enter the occupied side and locate the Caesar Terminal. Once that's determined, they will secure the room, deactivate Caesar and open the barrier door, letting the attacking force inside. They end the resistance and move everyone into safety."

The room was silent for a long moment before Gail nearly shouted, "That's absurd!"

Ms. Gilliard asked in a quiet but firm voice, "How will the team be able to make it to the airlock on that side?"

"In The Docks there are twelve mining suits in good working order, correct?" Hawk looked at Gates, who nodded. "The team will wear the suits and carry weapons and armor with them to the entrance."

Gail broke in, "We are in the lunar night, Major. It is nearly pitch black out there. The only light you'll have will be from the dome itself, and it won't be bright enough for you to safely travel on the surface."

"A point greatly in our favor." Forest picked up his explanation. "The team will be invisible to any lookouts the enemy has posted. Which would be highly doubtful anyway, but we always plan for any problem. Our night-vision goggles will fit under the mining helmets. The team will be tethered together, so they can lead each other."

Phelps asked, "What about the airlocks on this side? They aren't functional are they? I mean, the hangar door isn't functional."

To Hawk's surprise, it was Gail who answered this doubt. "The smaller airlocks have emergency manual functionality." She turned to explain to Hawk. "The airlock can function as an exit once only, allowing a single party through from the compound to the surface. But the lack of power means it cannot vent the chamber properly, so it will shut down and not allow return passage until power is restored. None of the other airlocks on this side will work to let your team back in, either. Once they go, they can't come back."

Hawk held her gaze. "We don't retreat, Administrator Moore. Once we go, we won't be coming back that way. We'll be coming back through the main corridor leading from the prisoners' cafeteria."

She opened her mouth to reply, fear filling her eyes, but Phelps was staring at the floorplan again and cut her off without realizing it. "But I gave you ten possible targets! What happens if it isn't the first one you check, or even the second or third? They'll find you. They'll hear you."

"That would be very unfortunate for them."

"Come on, Major! These are murderers. Gangbangers. Violent criminals. They aren't going to just throw their hands up and say 'Sorry, didn't mean to try and kill everyone. Please forgive us and send us back to our bunks.' They're going to kill you!"

Forest went rigid as the man spoke, and Hawk leaned forward, her fists on the table. She spoke in measured tones, "Mr. Phelps, was it? I appreciate your concern for our well-being." Several soldiers in the room stood a little straighter, crossing their arms. "But you aren't talking about the glorified mall cops you normally have protecting this place. You are talking about United States Army Special Forces. You are talking about the best fighting men and women who have ever breathed."

He looked a little cowed, but then Forest took a step forward. "This is Major Charlie Hawk, Mr. Phelps. She dropped into a shit storm in the mountains of Afghanistan with five men. They walked around for ten days, slitting the throats of two dozen of the most elite fighters the Taliban had and not a single one of them ever knew she was there. She put a bullet in the skull of five men before the first one hit the ground. She wears more medals to sleep than a whole division of Marines could earn in a lifetime. If she says she can walk around in the dark on the Moon to find one single computer among a thousand, pity the man who is sitting at that computer, you hear me?"

You could have heard a pin drop. To a person, the soldiers were grinning from ear to ear. The civilians looked like they would sleep with one eye open until these people left their station. Gail cleared her throat and looked pointedly at Hawk. "You're going out there?"

"I am the most experienced member of this company when it comes to incursion behind enemy lines. Without the exaggerations of my very dramatic captain, I am the best, and this mission cannot fail."

"Then I'm coming with you."

"Out of the question."

Gail put her fists on table, mimicking Hawk's posture. "You need a guide. Someone who can show you exactly where to go over there without fumbling around with these huge poster-size floorplans. That's me."

"No, it isn't."

"Major, she has a point."

Hawk's head snapped to face Forest, and he actually took a step back. "I said no, Captain!"

"Ma'am, with all due respect, you'll need someone familiar with the structure."

She pushed off the table, transferring her glare to the civilians but refusing to look at Gail. "Fine. I need the person who knows this station best. I'm assuming that would be Drumm or one of his men? How about you?" She pointed at the man in the denim shirt. "You're head of maintenance, right? You should know this place like the back of your hand."

The man looked sheepish and rubbed his neck. Hawk transferred her glare to Stephanie Gilliard. "I need a name."

She looked at Hawk and then away again. When she spoke, her voice was an octave higher than before, "Please, please don't shoot me, ma'am. The thing is…well…"

"A name!"

She jumped and pointed at Gail. Both of the men shrugged and did the same. Phelps was the only one who had the nerve to speak. "All of us have our areas that we know real well, but Ms. Moore knows this place better than anyone. If I had to pick someone to find their way around over there, it's her. She's been here longer than anyone else, and, to be honest, most of us are afraid to go over to the prisoners' side. She's the only one over there on a regular basis." After a brief pause he added, "Ma'am."

Gail's smile was infuriatingly smug.

CHAPTER TWENTY-SEVEN

The meeting broke up with people going in a dozen different directions. The chaos was organized, but barely. Gail lost track of Hawk somewhere in between a strained conversation with Stephanie Gilliard and a set of clipped instructions from a soldier the size of an oak tree. When she looked around the room, she found it nearly empty, and no one there had that authoritative set to their shoulders or choppy blond hair visible underneath their green beret. Gail remembered all too clearly the set of Hawk's jaw and the fire in her eyes as she set off. Something told her they needed to talk. The most likely place to find her was The Docks, so Gail headed off in that direction.

The lights had dimmed perceptively now, and only every other light in the main halls was glowing. Most of the less frequently used hallways and rooms were completely dark, making for an eerie trek. The mood would probably have struck her more had there not been several people in small groups dotted through the hall, deep in discussion. If not for those signs of human life, Gail might've stumbled out of her conference room into a graveyard. Up ahead was a pitch-black opening that led to a series of storage closets. Her body ached to avoid it, but she never got the chance to alter her course.

Just as she came level with the shadowy entrance, a cold hand shot out and wrapped around her arm just under her armpit, catching her in a ferocious grip. It nearly yanked her off her feet and darkness spun around her as she tumbled into the hallway. Her captor yanked back at the last second, setting her back against the wall rather than pushing her into it. The air shot out of her lungs and the grip around her arm tightened, making her breath come out in a yelp.

Bared teeth materialized out of the gloom inches from her eyes. "Just what the hell do you think you're doing?"

Her eyes were streaming and she fought for breath. "Hawk?"

"Are you trying to get yourself killed, is that it?"

"No, of course not!"

"Then what the hell are you doing?"

"I'm trying to help. I can help."

Hawk let go of Gail's arm, but didn't back off. "You aren't going. You're going to give me a verbal walkthrough, step by step, before I leave. You can be on comms with me in case something comes up, but you are not leaving this wing."

Her proximity was intoxicating, and Gail found herself staring at Hawk's lips rather than her burning eyes. Still, she would not be put off so easily. "No. I'm going with you. There are a million things that could go wrong, and I can't guide you if I'm not there."

"I'll be wearing a camera. You can see the feed. That'll have to be enough."

"I don't think that way. I need to be there. Besides, if you have to escape an attack, you don't need me shouting directions in your ear. What if I get turned around and send you the wrong way? You need me out there with you."

"It's too dangerous."

"I agree. You shouldn't be going at all, but since you are, I'm going too."

Anger boiled over inside Hawk. "You aren't a soldier, Gail! You'll just be in the way."

"I may not be a soldier, but I know this station better than anyone. Without me you'll just be a dead soldier."

"This is not a game, damn it!" She growled and turned away, staring at the opposite wall, her back heaving with each breath. Her voice sounded distant when she spoke again. "Abigail, you have a daughter. What if something happens to you?"

Fear gripped her heart like a vice. She hadn't thought of Lou-Lou when she spoke up in the conference room, but she thought of her now. Maybe her decision was selfish, or maybe it was the best thing for Lou-Lou. Whatever the answer, her mind was made up.

"My daughter has two mothers who love her very much. She'll be fine. I need to do everything I can to protect you now."

Hawk's face was incredulous. "I can protect myself."

"I know." She stepped forward and put a hand on Hawk's forearm. "I know you can. I just want to watch."

There was a beat of silence before Hawk laughed, a low, rolling, joyous thing that made Gail's face ache from smiling. Hawk shook her head. "You're ridiculous."

"I can honestly say no one has ever said that about me."

Hawk moved forward a fraction, their bodies almost touching. The honesty in her voice was raw, almost wounded. "Don't do this. Please?"

Gail took Hawk's hand, entwining their fingers and staring at the result. One hand dark and smooth, the other pale and rough. Hawk had a slashing scar across the back of her hand that shone brightest white in the dimness of the corridor. She wondered about its origins. A mark from one or another war or a childhood accident? Gail stared at that scar and knew she needed Hawk to live long enough to tell her the story. Needed it more than oxygen or light.

"My grandmother was born a rebel. She's the one who moved the family back to the reservation. Who reclaimed our culture after our ancestors abandoned it in favor of assimilation in the nineteenth century. She moved back to the Rez and she protested for Native rights and she married a full-blood Lakota man and she was as red as they come." She looked up at Hawk's half-smile curving her full lips. "But she had a secret obsession. Something so white and mainstream that she hid it even from my grandfather, but I was her special favorite and she shared it with me. James Bond."

Hawk squinted at her in the darkness. "What? Like the movies? Sean Connery?"

"Sean Connery. Roger Moore. She even liked the one with George Lazenby where he cried at the end." She started running her thumb over Hawk's palm. "She'd send the rest of the family off in a thousand different directions, then sit with me on the couch and pop in a tape."

"Sounds nice."

"It was. We'd watch those movies over and over. *Moonraker* was her favorite."

"That's the space one right? Appropriate. I think I saw it."

"I watched it with Unci thirty times at least. I haven't been able to watch it since she died, but I remember scenes from it all the time and the way she sighed over Roger Moore."

Gail focused on Hawk's hand for a moment, waiting for her sadness to pass. She hadn't thought of her grandmother in a long time. Apparently, whatever Hawk awoke in her last night was still affecting her. To her credit, Hawk let her sort through her emotions in silence.

"I would see these women. The Bond Women. They would sleep with him once and then be perfectly willing to die for him. There's one in *Moonraker*. The bad guy's secretary. She was impossibly skinny with legs for days and this beautiful long, black hair."

"I definitely remember her. She flew a helicopter or something."

"That's the one. She sleeps with Bond and then covers for him with her boss even though she knows he'll kill her for it. She does it anyway and the bad guy has his dogs rip her apart."

Gail felt Hawk's impatience, but she needed to explain it to herself almost as much as she needed to it explain it to her.

"I thought that was so ridiculous at the time. To throw away your life for someone you barely know just because of one night." She looked up into Hawk's eyes. "Maybe I understand her a little more now."

"Gail…"

"I don't want to die, Charlie." She moved her hand back up to Hawk's forearm, gripping hard at the thick fabric of her jacket. "But I'd risk anything for you."

"Why?"

"Because you would for me."

Hawk stared into her eyes and saw the determination there. "Fuck. I'm not going to be able to change your mind, am I?"

She took a step forward, closing the gap between them. "Not a chance."

Their lips were inches apart. Gail's eyes were closing. She could feel Hawk's breath on her lips. A burst of noise came from the main corridor, and they both jumped in unison.

"There you are!" Derek Drumm's irascible face wasn't the most alarming shade of red Gail had ever seen it, but his forehead was beaded with sweat. He came charging down the hall toward them, index finger outstretched, Forest marching along behind him.

"You!" He shoved his massive finger in Gail's face. She let go of Hawk's arm in surprise. "You! What the fuck is this I hear about how you're some goddamn expert on this station? You want to go in with the team on an attack mission? Are you out of your mind?"

Gail started to speak in response, but he shot her a dismissive look and waved his hand. He turned on Hawk. "And you! What are you thinking letting a civilian go along with you? A useless, corporate ass-kisser of a woman no less. She's got no place on that team."

Gail barely heard anything he said, the blood was pounding so hard in her ears. Fortunately, Forest was there to grab the man by the shoulder. "Mr. Drumm! I told you that the decision has been made. And, incidentally, I'd watch the disrespect. Major Hawk doesn't take too kindly to…"

"The time has passed for prettying this situation up, boy." He turned back to Hawk, this time shoving his finger into his own chest. "You need me on that team, Major. This is my base, no matter what she says. I run it. I protect it. I could find my way around it with my ass sewn over my eyeballs!"

Hawk put her hand up and he came to a wheezing halt. She looked past him at Forest who rolled his eyes and shrugged. Crossing her arms over her chest, she said, "While that's a lovely visual you've given all of us, the folks we consulted all agreed that the person with the best working knowledge of this facility was Ms. Moore."

"Her people backing her up!"

Gail tried to speak in her own defense, but Hawk got in first.

"Okay. Let's put it to the test." She pointed past him to the main corridor. "That corridor is blocked. Elevators are down and there is the potential for hostile presence in the main staircase at the end of the hall. Tell me how to get back to The Docks safely."

He took a long minute, his forehead wrinkling in concentration. "This hall leads to a series of offices. One big open room full of cubicles, so it provides tactical cover. At the far west side of that room is a maintenance room with a secondary stairwell. It runs behind the elevators for maintenance access and so it follows the same route. It puts out on the ground floor right beside the bank of elevators and you can follow the normal route back to The Docks."

Hawk turned her attention away from his smug face to Gail, who crossed her arms lazily, realizing from Hawk's face that she knew who'd pass the test.

"I take it you've never used that secondary stairwell, Derek? It's more like a series of ladders and open catwalks. The descent would be extremely slow, and, more importantly, it shares a wall with the main stairwell. If you've ever been in there when someone is on the other side it sounds like a herd of elephants passing through. The hostile presence in the stairwell would undoubtedly hear you all descending and would come investigate. You'd be sitting ducks on those ladders and you'd move far too slowly to outrun them."

She took a moment for that to soak in before continuing, "But if you follow the hall past the main office space to the far end, it dead ends at a series of storage rooms and the main bathrooms for the floor. It is the farthest northern point of the dome and there is another stairwell there. It is rarely used by anyone other than the people who have the apartments at the far end of the halls. It's also a stairwell that is not duplicated on the prisoner side. They have fewer access points to their dormitories, so they might not even know it exists. On the ground floor is the gym to your right and the library to the left. Head right past the gym and you'll dead end at The Docks."

Even Forest had a grin a mile wide. Hawk shrugged and went to move past Drumm. "Tough luck. The lady's coming with us."

He stuck out his hand and slammed it into Hawk's chest, stopping her roughly. "That was a bullshit test, and you know it. Not a chance in hell I'm letting her go with you."

It seemed a good time for Gail to intervene, even if it was difficult to keep the satisfaction out of her voice. "Derek, we really don't have time…"

He whipped his head around to her. "We're gonna make time. Now shut your mouth, love."

Gail wrinkled her nose. "Love?"

"Don't ruin your panties, girl, it's just an expression. You're not my type."

He turned to face Hawk again, and instead of her face, he found himself looking at her fist. It connected with his left cheek, just below his eye, and he dropped to the floor like a stone. He lay completely still where he fell, groaning.

"Shit, Charlie!" Forest was grinning at her like a kid who'd just watched his dad telling off his teacher. His eyes flickered to Gail and he hurried to say, "Sorry, I mean, Major. That was…"

"Unwise," She said, rubbing her knuckles and looking down at the pink flesh. "Still, it felt really fucking good. Captain, if you wouldn't mind, after he regains consciousness, could you find a small, dark room to lock him in? Somewhere near the secretary so we don't have to spare more soldiers to guard our growing list of prisoners. I'd rather not deal with him until this is over."

"Yes, ma'am. It will be my pleasure."

"I'm going to take Administrator Moore to the staging area to be fitted with a TAC vest and helmet. Get yourself down there on the double."

She didn't wait for his nod but took Gail's hand and guided her to the elevator. Forest followed into the hallway to get a few men to help him wake the Security Captain and caught a glimpse of Gail shoving his CO against the elevator wall and pulling her into a deep kiss before the doors slid shut.

CHAPTER TWENTY-EIGHT

Gail had spent three years of her life living on the Moon. She ran the place. She knew Moon Base intimately and could tell you the name and birthday and number of pets back home for every one of the corporate employees. The one thing she had not done, not once in her tenure, was walk on the surface. It wasn't that she was uninterested in the experience. In fact, she thought often what it would like to strap on one of the suits and go over to the site of one of the American flags the Apollo crews had left. Some of her more adventurous employees took the trip on their down time. She simply hadn't gotten around to it. Mainly because the idea terrified her and she had nightmares at least once a week about being trapped outside with no way back to safety.

She hadn't mentioned her fear to Hawk or to the soldier who walked her through donning her tactical vest and combat helmet. She hadn't mentioned it to Billy Summers, the mining support team member who called her "ma'am" because she was probably old enough to be his mother and who had helped her get into her space suit. She hadn't mentioned it to any of her employees who came to wish her luck before being locked in their apartments for their own safety.

Not talking about it had almost made it seem like the fear wasn't there. Right up until they stepped into the airlock and she heard the hiss of atmosphere leaking out and the alarm claxons wailing to tell them there was no going back now. If she hadn't been tethered to Hawk in front and two soldiers behind, she would have sprinted for the door and banged on it until her hands were bruised and bloody and her nightmare over.

Hawk had told her that it would be easier for her to not have night vision goggles. "You can't fear what you can't see." Maybe in Charlie Hawk's world you can't fear what you can't see. In Abigail Moore's world, however, she feared nothing but the things she couldn't see. Mainly because what she feared almost as much as the empty, asphyxiating void of space was the empty, lightless void of space. A dark so crushing that people who live in a world of sunlight every single day could have no idea the weight of blackness. There was no dark on Earth to compare. There was no dark that lasted two weeks and was always there, tickling at the edge of reality, ready to pop up again in another fourteen short days. The clock that blackness was always ticking, and the long lunar night was a nightmare that would always return.

For ten minutes the twelve of them hopped and bounced slowly through the limited gravity. Gail's fear had piled so high inside her that it was choking her. She couldn't take it anymore. She had to get out. She needed light and real air. Not this disgusting, canned air that tasted dead and dry like subway filth. But rather the air that blew a crisp, hot breeze across the mesas and gave her spirit life. Mostly, she had to get this fucking suit off so that she could take a deep breath. Her hand even started reaching for her face, or where she thought her face must be since she was so disorientated by her blindness.

"We're rounding the far side of the dome now." Hawk's voice sounded in her ear and immediately the recycled air in her mask was breathable again. "Should get some light in a few steps. Everyone okay back there?"

Gail didn't trust her voice, but a chorus of "yes ma'am" echoed in her ear. She remembered the tether between them and she pictured it, stretching out weightless in front of her. She could almost see it, hooked by a glinting metal clasp to the back of a suit that she knew contained the one woman who could calm her. It took a long moment for the truth to register in her panicked mind. She wasn't picturing the tether, she was seeing it. Faint and washed out of any color, but it was there, real and solid. Hawk was there too, bouncing like a kid in a jumping castle, strong arms pumping through the thin air. Arms that would catch her if she fell. Arms that were worth living for. Gail took a deep, rattling breath.

Looking up and off to her left Gail saw the glowing outline of their destination. The airlock entrance was painted bright yellow to draw the eye. To guide wanderers on the surface to sanctuary. Sanctuary from one fear, but full of another. The men inside were ruthless and drunk on power. They would kill her the moment they saw her. Red's words to Hawk echoed in her ears, requesting women be left behind for their amusement. Requesting that *she* be left behind. Killing her would be the best option. Perhaps it was the sight of the door, perhaps the realization that she had already faced her worst fear, perhaps it was simply seeing Hawk's form in front of her again. Whatever the cause, she finally felt ready to face the task ahead.

They had to be both quick and quiet getting into the airlock and switching from their mining suits to battle gear. They accomplished the task quickly, and Gail was reminded that these men and women were Special Forces. The legendary Green Berets. And she had spent the night with the best of them all. Perhaps she belonged here after all. She tried to catch Hawk's eye, but she was all business now. Her focus was on everyone and everything, and they would not step a foot out into danger until she was satisfied that everything was in order. That singular focus reminded Gail that she was not Bond. She was a Bond girl. And the Bond girls rarely lived to the end credits.

This is Forest. Strike Team One come in. You there Major?

Hawk put her finger to her ear. "I'm here, Captain. Team is in place."

Excellent. I've got eyes on, ma'am.

She turned and her eyes were like glaciers. "Moore, you're up front with me."

Ma'am, code names should be used in case our communications are intercepted.

Hawk shook her head and smiled, checking her weapon and replying in a low voice, "Fine, Captain. I know how much you like your games. Talk me through it."

Eagle is on point with Sacagawea.

"Forest!"

What?

There was snickering from several different voices and someone whispered, "That is so racist."

What? It makes sense.

"Jesus Fucking Christ, Forest. What the hell is wrong with you?"

Come on! Like I was the only one thinking it! Hot Indian chick guiding the white soldiers through hostile territory? What other handle was I supposed to use?

"Who's Sacagawea?"

"Crack a book every now and then, Morris. She's the chick on the dollar coins you get at the post office."

"I really don't think that's appropriate."

"The Major's totally gonna shoot him when we get back over there."

It is both easy to remember and historically accurate.

"I don't think you're supposed to call her Indian. I think Native American is the term."

"Everybody shut up!" Hawk's shouted whisper stilled the room. "You think this is a fucking joke, Forest? There are three bags in The Docks with good men inside. This is no fucking joke, soldier."

No, ma'am. Of course not, ma'am. I didn't mean to...

"Shut up, Forest." She closed her eyes and let out her breath slowly. "No handles. I don't care if they intercept our transmissions and know who we are. I will kill them if they get in my way. You just listen to our progress and report to the Bravo Team and Delta Team when to expect the door to be breached. Other than that, you keep your mouth shut, understood?"

Ma'am. Yes, ma'am.

"And Forest." A ghost of a smile crossed her lips. "Eagle? Really? That was the best joke you could come up with?"

Cause your name is Hawk. Get it? Hawk. Eagle.

"I get the joke, Forest. It's just not fucking funny, Captain."

Yeah, well, you aren't exactly known as the funny one in Charlie Company.

His voice sounded distinctly pouty to Gail, but she was in no mood to pity his humiliation. Hers was much greater.

Hawk signaled to the team over her shoulder and they fell into a double-line formation behind her. She pointed Gail forward before she replied to Forest's quip, "Nope. I'm the pretty one."

Gail led them through a few back corridors, peaking around corners and moving slower than may have been necessary. She was hyperaware of the fact that she was the only person without a gun. They had decided that the security substation at the entrance to the farming dome was the best place to start. It was the closest to their entry point but was also close enough to the prisoners to be one of the more likely spots. The team assumed that there would be at least a token guard in place, and there was a chance that either Red or someone he trusted highly would be at the terminal monitoring the battery drain.

The corridor leading to the substation office was empty, but the relatively bright lights and the stillness unnerved Gail. She'd become accustomed to the slowly dimming chill on the civilian side. She looked back at Hawk, who nodded and waved her team forward. Two pairs of soldiers advanced, moving in near-perfect synchronization down the hall. Their weapons moved constantly, scanning every nook and cranny, their heads and torsos moved with them as though they were physically attached. It was graceful, the way they swept down the hall, their knees bent, their arms tracing delicate arcs in the silence. They looked like they were dancing, and the movement mesmerized Gail. She leaned out into the hall to watch their progress, but Hawk slipped in front of her, blocking her line of sight.

"Keep behind me," she said in a loud whisper. "And keep your head down if you hear shots."

The four men arrived at a bank of windows separating the office from the corridor. They exchanged a series of hand signals that meant nothing to Gail. They nodded one by one and spread out in different directions, one in a crouch under the glass, another standing behind with weapon raised. They arrived at the security gate and took a moment to scan the area. The gate resembled the turnstiles at the entrance to a subway, with an arm that rotated as each person passed. It was used to both restrict access to the farming dome and also keep count of those coming and going. Four soldiers made quick work of the barrier, vaulting it in turns while the others remained vigilant. They dropped out of sight then, ducking into the office behind.

Hawk nodded to another pair, who moved down the hall, a little quicker this time, knowing the way was clear. The original four were dark shapes moving behind the glass, but it was impossible to tell what they were doing. There was a crackle in Gail's ear, and a voice she didn't recognize spoke.

All clear, Major. No terminals online and no hostiles. Looks like this isn't the place.

"It was too good to be true that we'd find it straight off." Hawk's voice was louder in Gail's earpiece than from her lips a foot away. "Fall back and we'll regroup."

Yes, ma'am.

She turned to Gail. "The kitchen office. Get me there."

The kitchen office was a bust, too. It was, however, much harder to get in and out quietly. Forest had informed them through their comms that the Beta and Delta Teams had begun the assault to create their diversion. Hawk sent a scout toward that action, but only far enough to see that the attack forced the group of prisoners without guns to the back of the cafeteria, too close for comfort to the strike team.

The safest move now was to leave most of Hawk's force far from the kitchen office while the scouts went ahead to check the computer. Hawk went with the scouts, since this was the most dangerous spot, and while she was gone, Gail found herself twisting the cuff of her workout jacket until it frayed. When Hawk's voice finally came through the speaker in Gail's ear she actually sighed in relief even though she confirmed that the hunt was still on.

They were all feeling the tension now. Despite their realism in the relative comfort of the conference room, every one of them had hoped to find the terminal quickly, Gail most of all. The longer it took to find, the less likely they would be successful. Gail felt their chances lessening with each passing second and worse, as guide, she felt the failure squarely on her shoulders. She needed this next location to be the one.

After slipping silently away from the kitchen, they made their way to the security station at the entrance to the livestock dome. It was an identical set up to the farming dome, but the farthest from the cafeteria. Everyone but Gail thought it was the least likely target. Forest had argued hard in their ears to go to other objectives first, but Gail was firm. Red worked in the livestock dome half of his shifts. He had seduced her secretary there. He had probably used the cover of the animal noises to plan the rebellion in the first place. She remembered seeing him in there, and she remembered him looking at ease. At home. If he was comfortable in that space, he was more likely to know it well and want to use it as his power center.

Hawk had trusted Gail's instincts, which felt like validation, but now they were nearing the corridor and everything was still frustratingly silent and deserted. Perhaps Red and his men were too busy fighting to protect the place? After all, who would imagine that they could get in here? They had taken back hallways and little-used corridors in their roundabout journey. Maybe they just hadn't seen the prisoners running toward the diversionary battle, abandoning an asset they had every reason to think was secure. Maybe it would be as easy as walking in and typing a few commands into the keyboard and the nightmare would be over. She even smiled a little at the thought. She was already planning their triumphant return, Red held at gunpoint, his hands over his head, a look of contrition on his no-longer smug face.

Then the fireworks started.

Ridiculously, that's what she thought it was. Fireworks. The popping, sizzling and crackling, and the people all around shouting their approval and admiration. Only there were no flashes of colorful light. The shouts were not of approval but of warning. Angry bees slammed into the walls, poking holes in the smooth, heather-gray surface. Hawk shoved Gail to her knees and then to her stomach. Some of the shouting was hers, and her gun opened up with a cavalcade of loud pops. Gail tried to shove her hands over her assaulted ears, but her fingertips banged painfully into the metal of her helmet. The plates in her vest, protecting her heart and lungs from enemy fire, pressed painfully into her breasts as she lay face down on the floor.

A hand grabbed the shoulder strap of her vest and the shouting in her ear got louder. Her first thought was that one of the prisoners had broken free, and they were trying to drag her away. She struggled with the arm trying to pull her to her feet, swatting at it and kicking her legs, blindly flailing. She wouldn't go to him without a fight.

"Gail! Gail, get up! Get up now!"

It was Hawk's voice. She stopped struggling to stay down, and now struggled to get up. The hand gripping her vest was pulling her awkwardly and she wished Hawk would let go so she could stand on her own. Her shoes squeaked on the tile floor as they finally got under her.

"Come with me! Stay close!"

Hawk kept a hand pressed firmly between Gail's shoulder blades as they ran down the hall, hugging close to the wall. That forced her into an uncomfortable half-crouch, but she ran as fast as she could. Hawk was always a step ahead of her, but she was within sight and that was enough to keep her focused.

She stared at her toes, watching the sparkle of the stone chips in the polished floor flash by. She found herself wondering why Andrus had decided to send the floor tiles up from Earth. It was the same builder's grade white tile ubiquitous to every public school across the United States. They used it because it was cheap and more visually appealing than plain concrete, but the expense in shipping such a banal building material into space seemed ludicrous to her all of a sudden.

Gunfire burst into her thoughts and she found herself laughing. Giggling uncontrollably. She screamed at her brain to stop the laughter, that it was inappropriate and ridiculous, but she couldn't control it.

Hawk shoved her through a break in the wall, abruptly cutting Gail's hysterical laughter. She stumbled a few steps down a deserted hall, but at least she was finally able to stand. Distance muffled the sound of gunfire, and she looked around to get her bearings. Hawk stood at the entrance to the hall, her back pressed against the wall, her weapon held ready in front of her. As Gail watched, she dropped low and whipped around the corner, firing several pulses before sliding back behind to safety. Gunfire erupted from far away and a puff of pulverized plaster swirled from the corner. Hawk flinched back from the impact and then eased back to her position. She looked down the hall at Gail, her chest heaving but her face relaxed. Her lips moved, but a flurry of gunfire swallowed the words. Gail took a few steps forward, shaking her head.

Hawk waited for the firing to stop and then said quickly, "Get us out of here. Now."

Gail looked at the walls around her, but her mind went blank every time she heard a gun fire.

Hawk popped out from cover again, firing off three blasts in quick succession before dipping back behind the wall. The responding bullets came faster this time, slamming into the wall beside her within milliseconds of her moving back to safety.

"Gail! We need to get to that terminal. Now! Talk to me."

Her brain finally caught up with the moment. "This hall leads to prisoner locker rooms. A place for them to change and shower after they leave the livestock dome. There's only the one entrance to the locker room, so I don't think we can get in there, but further down the hall is a storage room. It's got a code lock. I don't remember what's in there, but there are two doors. We can get back to the main corridor from there and circle back around to the security station from behind."

"Do you know the code?"

"I think so."

"You think so?"

"We only use about a dozen codes. I don't know which one the door uses, but I know all the codes." She bit her bottom lip and stared at the floor, working her way through the index of numbers flying in front of her eyes. "I don't think they'd have any reason to change them. I can get us in."

Hawk dropped her rifle to point at the floor and marched past her. "Let's go. We need to hurry."

"What about the rest of the team?"

"They can hold this position, cover for us while we complete the mission."

Hawk started shouting instructions into her comms, but it all felt wrong to Gail.

"Wait!" She stopped in her tracks and pointed back the way they had come. "We need to help them."

Hawk spun and marched back toward her, stopping when they were separated only by their breath. "We *are* helping them. They'll hold this position and keep Red occupied while we go open those doors. This is almost over, Gail. Don't lose it now, okay?"

She swallowed hard. It was written all over Hawk's face. If Gail's instinct was to stay and help when she didn't have the least ability to do so, it must have been exponentially worse for Hawk who had the training and weaponry Gail lacked. She nodded and Hawk turned without a word, checking the way ahead for resistance. They were both rigid with tension as they moved through the deserted halls, the sound of gunfire muffled but always present through the walls. Their path was clear straight through to the storage room door, and Hawk stood back to cover her while she punched in codes.

Gail had always had a head for numbers. It was one of the things that had drawn her to the business world. In meetings she could rattle off statistics and risk formulas and projected profits from memory. She still remembered the full ten-digit bank account number that her mother opened for her when she was twelve years old. What was more, the pressure of a deadline had always clarified her thinking. The moment she'd seen the door and the heat-activated keypad under the handle, she'd determined the most likely code to unlock it.

The memory she had of that storage room was of boxes. The same generic cardboard boxes they used for nearly every type of storage throughout the base. It could be anything from files of two-year-old time sheets to live ammunition. This close to a security substation, she would think that it would be security storage. But then they were close to the prisoner locker room, so it could be soap.

She mumbled to herself as she typed. "Pound, four, eight, four, zero, star. Not it. Okay, pound, two, one, two, zero, star. Nope."

A series of cheery electronic beeps sounded after the third attempt. She looked up at Hawk, her face beaming, but the soldier did not make eye contact. Her body was rigid and her focus entirely on the empty corridor behind them. Gail's smile faltered and she slammed her palm down on the door handle. It clicked open and the lights flicked on.

The stacked boxes she remembered came into view. Hawk backed into the room and closed the door behind them. Then she turned, sweeping her weapon in a precise arc as she scanned the room. Gail did not wait for her to finish her inspection, but rather hurried across to the door at the far end of the wall to her left.

"Wait." Hawk moved forward with measured steps. "Let me open it. What's on the other side?"

"A short hall with three doors. One at the far end and two on the right. We're heading for the one directly across from this one. That leads to a longer hall with a corridor off on the left wall about two-thirds down."

"How far?"

"Maybe twenty yards to corridor. There are two corridors on the right. One about ten yards down, and the other a bit further on. There is a jog to the right at the end. We follow that. It ends at the back door of the livestock security station."

"Okay." Hawk put her ear to the door for a long moment, then pulled it back. "We go slow. Stay behind me."

Tension ate away at Gail. Hawk insisted on checking every door they passed for noises beyond and made Gail stop as they approached every hallway to clear it before waving her to continue.

The trip from the storage room to the back door of the security station felt like it had taken hours, and the sound of gunfire came closer and closer with each step. When they arrived at the final door, Hawk took even longer than usual listening for movement and checking behind for anyone approaching. She even called to her squad for an update, but they either could not hear her or were not in a position to answer. Forest was similarly indisposed, involved in liaising with those assaulting the main door as a distraction, but he at least took a moment to scream at Hawk to get a move on.

Hawk's face was tight with worry, but Gail could not stay still any longer. She reached forward and entered the code quickly enough to avoid being stopped. Hawk cut her an angry look, popped the door handle and grabbed her weapon again with lightning-fast precision. She pointed at the threshold as a warning for Gail to remain there and moved off to clear the room.

They entered behind a bank of servers stacked neatly on metal shelves. An empty desk to the left had a few discarded tools on it and nothing else. Hawk stepped around the shelves, moving slowly and peering through gaps in the rows of humming machines. Tiny, multicolored LED lights blinked continuously and Gail was reminded of the server room on the lowest floor of offices, just above her apartment. She wasn't an electronics expert but she thought these may be servers dedicated to surveillance, given their location.

Hawk moved around another bank of shelves and Gail couldn't see her any more. She had a moment of panic, feeling exposed, and rushed to catch up. The door banged shut behind her and she winced at the sound, magnified by the empty room and the heightened tension.

When she rounded the corner of shelves, she was staring down the barrel of a gun. Her hiccup of surprise was cut short by Hawk's palm closing over the lower half of her face as she lowered her gun. The woman's eyes bore into her, and she slowly removed her hand, bringing a finger to her lips in a plea for silence. Gail nodded, her helmet banging forward slightly on her loose chin strap.

Hawk turned and moved back to the corner of the shelves, peering around it. Apparently she didn't see anything, because she moved on, rolling her boots from heel to toe soundlessly. Gail followed closely.

The room opened up over Hawk's shoulder. The banks of electronic equipment were replaced by a wall of monitors, each displaying the fixed image of a security feed inside the dome. Cows chewed cud, chickens flapped around noiselessly and tools hung abandoned on pegboard walls. To the left was a wall of windows, looking out on an empty hall and the same subway turnstiles they had seen before.

There were no men visible, but the sound of shouting and guns was much louder here. They had to be nearby. In the center of the room was a trio of desks, each facing a different direction, though none backed up to the wall of windows. The monitor facing them was black as the space outside, and, though she couldn't see it, the lack of light on the opposing desk indicated that that computer was also off. The desk to the right, however, the one facing the glass, was illuminated by a blue glow.

Gail's whisper was harsh and strained, even to her own ears. "That's it!"

She brushed past Hawk's shoulder, knocking her unintentionally off-balance as she raced toward the Caesar Terminal.

"Gail! Don't!"

She realized her mistake just as Hawk called out to her, but it wasn't the words that convinced her. Instead, it was the lithe form that stepped out from behind a bookshelf on the right wall and leveled the barrel of a handgun directly between her eyes.

"I was hoping she'd bring you, Administrator Moore." Red's arm shot out and wrapped around her neck, twisting her around and slamming her back against his chest. The rest of his words came in a silken whisper right beside her ear, "I've been *aching* to see you again."

CHAPTER TWENTY-NINE

The barrel of his pistol was ice cold as it pressed against the soft flesh of her neck. He pushed it against her jugular, and her pulse strained against the pressure. His body against her was sinewy and bony, his arm around her chest like a band of iron, his slim fingers biting into her shoulder.

"I don't particularly like this look for you, Gail. May I call you Gail?" He didn't wait for an answer but kept talking as he released her shoulder and unbuckled her helmet. He tossed it aside, the metal clattering loudly on the concrete floor, and the gun still pressed hard against her neck. "It's too butch for you. I like the power suits. The tight skirts. The tall heels. You have such nicely defined calves. You should keep showing them off. And your hair. Take it down from the ponytail, dear."

Her arms felt too weak to move, and she couldn't raise her eyes to look at Hawk, even though she saw her boots rooted to the floor in front of her.

"I said take your hair down!"

His shout echoed in her ear, and she winced with the pain of it. She lifted her left hand and gripped at the rubber band holding her hair in place. With the gun pressed to the right side of her neck, she was afraid to move too much, so she yanked at it awkwardly.

"That's nice," He said, and her lip curled as he buried his nose into her scalp. "I like it when a woman wears her hair down. Don't you, Major?"

Gail finally gathered the strength to look up at Hawk. Her eyes were cold as ice and fixed, not on her, but on Red. She'd seen that look before. In the eyes of Roger Moore and Sean Connery. Given the choice, Bond always took out the bad guy at the expense of the Bond girl. She was the Bond girl again, and she could feel the end credits cueing up.

"Let her go and I won't kill you."

He laughed. It wasn't the low, evil chuckle of a sinister mastermind, but the high-pitched, hyena giggle she had heard through Hawk's body mic. He pulled her tight against him and ran his calloused thumb over the skin of her neck. His thick fingernail clicked against the barrel of his gun and then slid away, making her skin crawl. Click, slide, click, slide, and still he stared at Hawk without a word.

His lips were at her ear again. "Take off the vest, sweetheart. Very...very...slowly."

She tried not to let her fingers tremble as she reached for the Velcro tabs. She kept her eyes on Hawk as she peeled them back, the tearing noise making her eyes prickle. Hawk never even glanced at her. Her gaze was through the sights of her rifle, and the rifle was pointed at his head. Gail released the last fastener, the one on her left shoulder, and he shifted his body back so that she could slip out of it. She dropped it to the ground next to her and felt suddenly freezing cold. His body pressed against her again and she could feel his bony shoulder against her through the thin polyester of her compression shirt. She closed her eyes to cut out the image of Hawk not looking at her.

"Very good." His voice moved away from her ear. "Now, Major Hawk, if you decide to take your chances and fire at us, I think you know what'll happen, don't you?"

"It's over, Red. My men are cutting through the barrier door and they'll come swarming here like a pack of fucking locusts. You're done. Why don't you make it easier on yourself and put the gun down?"

His breath tickled her ear and he started the slow rub of his thumb on her neck again. "She's confident, isn't she, Gail? But you and I know she's bluffing. The attack on the cafeteria is a diversion. They cut a small hole and are firing through, but they won't get any farther than that. It would take a week to get through that door. And you don't have a week." He pulled her tight and his wide belt buckle pressed against the small of her back. "No, you both know that you don't have a chance. So, Major, unless you want me to disfigure this pretty face here, you're going to put your gun down behind you on the floor."

"Not a chance, Red."

His arm was gone from around her chest, but the gun pressed harder against her. Her eyes flew open and she saw that Hawk's eyes were not on his face any more. They were looking at Gail's left hand where it hung loose at her side. There was a sound like a shovel dragging along a sidewalk. It didn't make the slightest sense until the press of cold metal against her arm made her jump.

"Careful, Gail. It's *very* sharp. You wouldn't want me to hurt you, now would you?"

The knife blade slid up her arm as she held perfectly still. Then over her shirt sleeve and the prick of a needle point touched her chin. She didn't dare swallow or even breathe as it sat there, twisting against the point of her jaw. Then it slid away, down the column of her throat. The touch was light now, soft as a lover's caress as it passed over the slope of her breast and down to her belly. He laid it across her stomach, the tip at the mound of one hipbone, his fist where it gripped the hilt brushing against the other. She risked looking down at it and was appalled by the sight. It was huge and gleaming in the low light of the office. Massive and curved and deadly looking like something out of a horror film.

There was a rattle of metal and she looked up to see Hawk crouching down, one hand in the air, depositing her rifle on the floor behind her right heel. She stood slowly, her eyes back on his face and her jaw wide and clenched.

"I knew you'd see reason." She could feel his smile against her cheek. "And the sidearm. Nice and slow."

Her hand moved gracefully in slow motion. She unbuckled the holster and reached for the butt of the gun with two gloved fingers, angling her body so he could watch her. His smile widened as she plucked the gun out and held it in front of her, suspended between her thumb and middle finger. She turned to put it behind her but stopped as he spoke up.

"No, no. That's a little too easy." He looked around the room. "Put it in front of you and kick it over there. Toward the windows."

She did as he said and straightened. Reaching for the chin buckle of her helmet, she released it, taking off the helmet and tossing it aside without being asked. Then she removed her vest and dropped it, crossing her arms across her unprotected chest and staring him down.

"So accommodating. How nice."

"Let her go, Red. You and I can settle this together. You don't need her."

His laugh came again, tearing through the few nerves Gail held intact. She shuddered and he squeezed her tighter to him. "Ah, but you remember, Major Hawk. She's the one I want. Not you."

"You and I both know I can be a lot more fun than her."

Gail's rational mind told her that the leer in Hawk's voice was affected, but her heart stung briefly at the words and she felt her cheeks flush.

"Mmm...I'd wondered if she'd given it up to you. I've had suspicions about her, but she's been such a good girl while she's been up here. Not a single whisper of impropriety. You must be something special." The knife left Gail's belly as Red pressed down hard on both of her shoulders, turning her to face him as he did. Her knees buckled and she fell hard onto the floor, catching herself with her hands and struggling back up to an unpleasantly awkward kneel. "I do enjoy a woman on her knees. You too, Major. On your knees."

She didn't budge, didn't look down at Gail even as the barrel of the gun pressed into her head. "I've had guys ask me to do that before. What do you think my answer always is?"

The shots were so sudden, so unexpected that Gail didn't even feel the barrel gone from her head, until from the corner of her eye, she saw Hawk spin in her boots. She didn't cry out, but her hand went to her left bicep and twin streams of red poured between her fingers.

"On your knees or the next two will blow out your pretty little kneecaps."

Hawk staggered a little but straightened and threw her chest out once she was down. Gail could feel the tears running down her cheeks. The knife slipped quietly back into its sheath on his hip. His fingers were in her hair, grabbing a fistful and using it to wrench her head back painfully to look up at him.

Red didn't laugh. Didn't speak. He raised the gun to his face, turning it lovingly in the air in front of him. He put his nose close to the barrel and sniffed loudly. His lips turned up and his teeth gleamed in his grin.

"God, I've missed this!" He lowered the gun and looked across the room at Hawk on her knees. "It's the little things, ya know Major. The little things you took for granted in life that you miss desperately when you're locked up. The things you should have savored in the moment. If you had it to do all over again, you'd give them the loving respect they deserve."

His eyes went back to the gun and he twisted it in front of his eyes, yanking Gail's head back even harder and causing a sob to escape her lips.

"For some guys it's drugs. Or booze. Or whores. For me it's this." He threw his arm out in a grand gesture. "The smell of fresh blood and hot gunmetal. The sound of a woman crying, about to beg for her life. I can almost taste your death, Major. And it tastes so goddamn good."

His arm was still outstretched, the pistol pointed uselessly at the ceiling. Hawk wasn't far away, but too far if he saw her coming. Gail could taste her death, too, and it was bitter on her lips. If she didn't move now, she'd die with that bitter taste of Hawk's last moments on her tongue. She couldn't let that happen. She couldn't watch the woman she loved die.

There it was. The truth apparent to her because of a simple errant thought. She did love Hawk. It didn't make sense but it was true nonetheless. The realization was both sweet and hollow, given their predicament. She needed to do something. Her hand moved toward the knife before she planned to do it.

She reached out and her mind went blank. She had her fist wrapped around the hilt of the knife at the back of his belt. He looked down at her as she yanked it free. She didn't have to move her arm far, and then she had it buried in his back, just above the thick leather belt. He yelled and the gun came down, not to point at her, but the broad side hard against her cheek.

Her right eye exploded in white lights and she felt the concrete floor come up to smash into her shoulder. The room spun and her vision blurred. Time moved very strangely and sound didn't cooperate like it should. Shouting was all around her and even behind her, warped into new, strange voices. The pounding of boots echoed and duplicated. There was a warm trickle down the side of her face. It ran into her eye and stung. Hawk had one hand around Red's throat, one around his wrist. His arm still moved, though. The hand wrapped around his wrist was bright red. Gail blinked and the world shuddered. Bile charged into her throat. There was a sound like glass shattering.

There were three loud explosions. Her own scream deafened her. Then the world went black.

EPILOGUE

Gail stood at the wide window, soaking in the warmth of the sun on her shoulders and back. The strength of it clung to the fabric of her suit, soaking through to the silk blouse beneath and making her sweat. Within a moment, the sharp smell of recycled air blasted through the vent over her desk, drying the sweat in a frigid gust. She paced across the face of the window, shoulder turned to block the glare on her tablet, moving in and out of the air current.

Her phone chimed an incoming message, breaking her concentration and her stride. With a muttered curse, she marched to her desk and snatched up her cell.

Have you looked out the window yet today?

A smile crept across Gail's lips.

Of course I have

Liar

Fine- I'll go look now

That's my girl

Gail did go to the window, but she kept her eyes on the small screen. *That's my girl.* It'd been so long since she'd been anyone's anything. The simple words sent a jolt through her stomach that was half joy, half anxiety. When she finally wrenched her eyes away from the phone, the office view gave her the same strange mix of emotions. After three years avoiding ever-present windows and the terrible landscape they showed, she'd almost forgotten what it was like to see a beautiful world outside.

From the tenth floor of the Hamilton-Essex office building on Connecticut Avenue NW she could see the green grass and trees of Farragut Square. If she strained her eyes she could almost make out Lafayette Square and the White House beyond. More than that, she could see cars. She could see food carts, buses and most incredible of all, people walking around in the wide open. People who didn't have to wear suits to protect them from the insubstantial atmosphere. They could walk out their front doors without fear of suffocation and freezing death. As she watched them go about their lives as though it was the most natural thing in the world, Gail wondered when she would join them in that carefree life. When the joy of it would all be taken for granted.

There was a soft tap at the door and Gail turned to see her secretary slip timidly into the room. Short, thin and wildly efficient, Connie hadn't always been so nervous when entering this office. Not long after Gail started her new position, Connie walked in to find her immersed in research. Distracted, Gail looked up to see Beatrice's face on this stranger's body. As hard as she tried to apologize for her response, she knew Connie had been troubled by Gail's flash of fear and revulsion. She'd been quiet and hesitant ever since.

"Sorry to disturb you, Ms. Moore," Connie said, her shoulders hunched and her fingers tapping absentmindedly at the calendar in her hand. "Your three o'clock appointment is here."

Gail didn't need to consult her own copy of today's schedule, she'd memorized it the night before, as had been her habit for many years. She'd found, however, that Connie felt more at ease when she thought of Gail as little better than helpless, and so she allowed her secretary to introduce the reporter waiting outside.

"Thank you, Connie," Gail replied, checking her watch and noting with approval that the reporter was ten minutes early. "Show her in."

Gail had intended to remain standing as her guest entered, but she found suddenly that gravity was too much. She'd arrived back on Earth a little over six months ago, and yet she was still having trouble adjusting to life "planetside." The final days she'd spent on the colony had left her with recurring nightmares, and the legacy of three years in reduced gravity was recurring fatigue. The doctors, all provided grudgingly at Andrus's expense, had all assured her the weakness was not permanent and she intended to prove them correct.

The reporter, surprisingly young, was charming with a natural ease in interviewing. She introduced herself with only her first name, Helen, and gave Gail a firm handshake. With tawny skin, long braids down her back, and eyes that were soft and shrewd in equal measure, she started the interview with a few easy questions about Gail's education and experience. She managed this while somehow skirting her time at Andrus, which was impressive. Gail's career prior to her current position at The Humanity Project had begun and ended at that one corporation. Gail knew the questions would come, of course, but she had welcomed the brief reprieve.

Gail knew the interview was necessary. Her story was too good to ignore given the colossal disaster of Moon Base. The rebellion and its aftermath had occupied headlines around the globe for weeks. She had been featured in most of that coverage, particularly when she testified before Congress and then again at Beatrice's trial. Stone had spared them all a third round with some twisted bedsheets from his jail cell. His defiant suicide note was all the reporters had to talk about. Gail had taken this job partly to add her now well-known name to the cause of American prison reform. Her new employer had been patient with her thus far, but it was time she started earning her paycheck.

"Can you tell me about the work you're doing here? What is The Humanity Project?" Helen asked.

"It's a nonprofit organization dedicated to reform of the criminal justice system in America. We are working to end mass incarceration and racism in the judicial system that sees people of color jailed at astronomical rates. Most importantly, we want to be sure a safe, humane environment is provided for people who do find themselves behind bars."

Gail took a deep breath and shot a glance over to the framed photo on her desk. Lou-Lou smiled back at her, but she wasn't the pigtailed girl with missing baby teeth who had smiled at her from her desk on the Moon. Lou-Lou was three years older, with thinner cheeks and fewer freckles across her nose. That smile—her daughter's smile—gave her strength.

"As to what I'm doing here... I'm here because I had an uncomfortably close view of what an inhumane prison looks like. I tried on a person-to-person level to change lives, but I didn't have the power to effect real change. I'm here to make sure that what happened on Moon Base never happens again."

Hunger was palpable in the reporter's face, but she managed to hold her voice steady when she said, "Since you mention your time at Andrus, many people find it strange that you're advocating for prisoners' rights given the violence you experienced on the Moon."

"The violence was a direct result of the poor treatment those men endured. I don't condone their actions, but I understand their feeling of helplessness. They felt exploited because they were being exploited."

To her credit, Helen didn't devolve into the usual arguments. Those that claimed giving prisoners comfort and fair treatment equated somehow to appeasement or rewarding crime. As though cable television was sufficient incentive for a person to relinquish their freedom. Unfortunately, that meant she moved her questions to the more personal aspects of Gail's ordeal.

"There was a very public falling out between you and your former employer after the events on Moon Base. Can you tell me about that?"

"There isn't much to tell that hasn't already been reported. Andrus alleged breach of contract when I refused to remain at the colony. I made it clear that I would not put myself or my employees at further risk by staying. Nor would I allow what amounts to the enslavement of a workforce without a thorough reevaluation."

"So you don't feel it's appropriate that they've reopened the facility?"

"Certainly not."

"Even though they've made safety improvements?"

"All the changes Andrus have made were to benefit the civilian workforce at the expense of the prisoners. Increased security personnel, monitoring devices, restricted communication between the civilian and incarcerated populations. The environment was less than ideal when I was there, now it can only be described as inhumane."

Helen looked as though she wanted to argue, but she quickly checked her watch and changed tack with practiced nonchalance. "Why did you decide to return from the colony with the soldiers? Major Hawk's injuries were quite severe. Did that factor into your decision?"

Gail bought time by looking back at the photograph on her desk. Not at Lou-Lou this time, but the face of the woman hugging her. Seeing the smile on Hawk's face there, you'd never know how close she'd come to death. A series of images flashed through Gail's mind, bringing with them a shadow of the gut-wrenching fear of that last encounter with Red. Watching fire erupt from the muzzle of his pistol. The way Hawk's eyes glazed over as blood poured out of her. If her soldiers had been even a few seconds later, if the shootout that left Red unquestionably dead had gone differently, if Nguyen had tried to prolong treatment rather than insisting she return to Earth. Any tiny alteration and Gail would have been standing alone in Arlington Cemetery holding a folded flag.

"The situation was unsafe for both my staff and the prisoners under my care. It was prudent to evacuate."

The reporter leaned forward, "But off the record, you really came back for Major Hawk."

"I'm not going off the record."

"There are a lot of rumors about your relationship. The two of you haven't exactly been hiding it. Not that I can blame you. She's a pretty big deal at the Pentagon. There are rumors of an assignment to the National Security Council."

"She wasn't at the Pentagon then."

"No, but she was just as hot as she is now." Helen winked and asked, "When did you fall for her?"

"I definitely want to hear your answer to that one," came a familiar, teasing voice from the door.

Hawk looked just as smug in her uniform now as she had when she marched off a plane into Gail's life, but there was a lightness to her now that they weren't wrapped in a professional relationship. She leaned on the cane that would be a part of her life for some time to come, and managed to make even that gesture of dependence look strong. She winked at Gail in a very different manner than the reporter had. One that sent a thrill of anticipation through Gail's limbs.

"I thought this was an interview for *The Washington Post*," Hawk said. "These questions sound more *People Magazine* to me."

"It's a human interest story," Helen replied, holding out a hand for Hawk to shake. "People love the two of you. American heroes falling in love and saving lives. It'll bring in the readers."

Gail stood, collecting her bag and coat. "If the story of our relationship brings awareness to the issues I'm promoting here than so be it."

"I'm glad that's your attitude." Helen stood and tucked away her notebook, though it was with reluctance. "If I had a few more questions for you…"

Gail slipped her hand around Hawk's arm, smiling up into her sparkling eyes before responding, "I'll be happy to answer any follow-up questions, but it will have to be another day."

Hawk turned and they walked away together out into the green world and the bright hot sunshine.

Bella Books, Inc.

Women. Books. Even Better Together.

P.O. Box 10543
Tallahassee, FL 32302

Phone: 800-729-4992
www.bellabooks.com

CPSIA information can be obtained
at www.ICGtesting.com
Printed in the USA
BVHW030012120819
555643BV00001B/25/P